A Second Chance at Love

Karen Pless Gaines

Published by Karen Pless Gaines Toccoa Georgia,
karenplessgaines@outlook.com

ISBN: 979-8-9879003-7-6

DEDICATION

This is dedicated to the women who have learned to trust again, to open their hearts to the possibility of new love, and to embrace the joy that awaits them on the other side of grief. Your courage is inspiring, your vulnerability is breathtaking, and your willingness to love again is a testament to the enduring power of hope.

And to the women who have found love again, after loss, after heartbreak, after years of solitude—this book is a tribute to your newfound happiness, a celebration of second chances, and a testament to the enduring power of love to heal and to transform lives. Your story is a reminder that even in the deepest darkness, there is always the promise of a new dawn, a fresh start, and the possibility of a love that endures. May your journey inspire others to embrace their own healing, to find their own strength, and to open their hearts to the infinite possibilities that lie ahead. May this book serve as a gentle reminder that healing is possible, happiness is attainable, and love, in all its forms, is truly enduring.

ACKNOWLEDGMENTS

With heartfelt gratitude, I acknowledge the unwavering support and encouragement of my family and friends throughout the writing of this novel. Their belief in my work, even during moments of self-doubt, fueled my perseverance. Special thanks to my critique partners, whose insightful feedback sharpened the narrative and deepened the characters. I am also indebted to my daughter, whose patience and guidance brought this story to life. Finally, I offer my deepest appreciation to all those who have shared their stories of loss and healing; your courage and resilience inspired this book.

.

ACKNOWLEDGMENTS

CHAPTER 1

The scent of lavender and chamomile hung faintly in the air, a gentle whisper cutting through the heavier aroma of stale grief that clung to the corners of Lora Bennett's small cottage. Sunlight filtered through lace curtains, casting playful patterns on the polished wooden floor, illuminating dust motes that danced like tiny sparks of life in the stillness. It had been two years. Two long, heart-wrenching years since the vibrant laughter of Dawson, her husband, had echoed through these rooms. Two years since his strong arms had enveloped her, making her feel safe in a chaotic world. Two years since everything had shattered, leaving her adrift in a relentless sea of sorrow.

Now, silence reigned—a profound, suffocating silence that pressed against her chest, a heavy mirror to the emptiness hollowing out her heart. Lora had meticulously organized every corner of her home. The kitchen, flawlessly organized, the living room, painstakingly arranged, the pristine bedroom—all stood as reminders of her desperate struggle to maintain some semblance of control, to build a fortress against her fragile emotions. Yet, the carefully constructed façade was beginning to crumble. The weight of her grief, once subdued, loomed over her with relentless force, threatening to engulf her.

Her routine had become a rigid structure, a self-imposed prison designed to keep the pain at bay. Each day unfolded with predictable precision, a choreographed dance around the gaping wound in her soul. Mornings began with a quiet cup of tea and a chapter of Scripture, a ritual that offered fleeting moments of peace. Then came the women's ministry—her refuge, her purpose, her anchor in the stormy sea of her grief. She poured her heart into helping other women navigate their struggles, offering comfort and hope when they needed it most. In those moments, she was a beacon of light, a safe harbor in the tempest of their lives. But in pouring herself into others, she was neglecting the most important person: herself.

Every Tuesday and Thursday, Lora would take a deep breath, steady herself, and step outside to greet the ladies. She put on her best smile, one that she hoped would mask the turmoil she felt inside. Each grin was a façade, a brave attempt to hide the pain that still clung to her, relentless and bruising.

Without Dawson, her world had dimmed, and she felt like a ship adrift at sea. They had woven their lives together, sharing dreams, laughter, and the mundane moments that made life rich. Now, with him gone, Lora found herself in a vast emptiness—a gaping void she struggled to fill. Each day was a quest to reclaim a piece of herself, to navigate life without the anchor that was Dawson. She couldn't help but search for fragments of their past in every corner, wishing for just one more moment, one more shared smile.

Evenings were the hardest. The silence was deafening, a stark contrast to the comforting hum of Dawson's presence that once filled these rooms. Lora often found herself by the window, watching the tranquil lake as the sun dipped below the horizon, painting the sky in vibrant hues of orange, purple, and gold. The beauty of nature was bittersweet, revealing the stark contrast between the serenity outside and the chaos within her heart. The lake, once a cherished spot for peaceful walks and shared laughter with Dawson, had turned into a vast expanse of cold isolation, reflecting the desolation that had taken root deep within her soul.

Her cottage, once a haven of warmth and love, had devolved into a sterile sanctuary—an intricate museum of her loss. The furniture stood resolutely in place, photographs and mementos of Dawson carefully arranged, hinting at the joy that once filled the space. But now, there lingered a hollowness, an absence that no amount of dusting or tidying up could ever truly fill.

Lora couldn't bring herself to change a thing since Dawson left. His favorite button-up shirts remained folded with care in the drawers, while the rest hung in the closet, each piece a reminder of his presence. The living room table still held his well-worn Bible and journals, pages filled with thoughts and dreams he would never share again. Even his watch sat on the nightstand, a silent companion to the empty space beside her in bed.

Every corner of the house whispered his name, and the weight of letting him go felt insurmountable. The memories flooded back, each item sparking a bittersweet nostalgia. How could she move forward when it felt like she was clinging to the past? In the quiet moments, Lora found herself lost in the echoes of their laughter and plans, grappling with the ache of loss. Letting go felt like erasing a piece of herself, and she wasn't ready for that, not yet.

Lora's faith, once an unwavering pillar of strength, felt distant and obscured, shrouded by a cloud of grief and self-reproach. She prayed, of course, but those prayers often came laden with unanswered questions, served with an unsettling feeling of a God who seemed remote, uncaring, and even cruel. While certain passages of Scripture offered glimpses of comfort and hope, the solace she sought so desperately often eluded her, leaving her wrestling with doubts and uncertainty. Would her faith ever regain its former strength? Would the peace and joy she once cherished ever return to her?

Then there was Ethan, he had always been their pride and joy—their only child, a beacon of hope in a world that sometimes felt too quiet. Lora and Dawson had dreamed of a bustling home filled with the sounds of children's laughter, but fate had other plans. When Ethan went off to college, he met Ava, a vibrant soul who instantly captured his heart. It was as if the universe had conspired to bring them together; they were simply meant to be.

After graduation, the couple tied the knot and embarked on a new adventure, relocating to Texas, leaving behind their small-town roots in Georgia. They called often, their voices crackling over the phone, sharing snippets of their busy lives filled with careers and the joys of parenthood. Lora cherished these moments, especially hearing about the mischief of Ethan and Ava's three children—twin boys Aiden and Noah, who were as energetic as they were mischievous, and sweet little Megan, whose laughter was as bright as the summer sun.

Yet, as much as she longed to be closer to them, to wrap her arms around those three precious kids and create new memories together, Lora felt a tug at her heart. The women's ministry she led had become her second family. They relied on her for support and healing, and the thought of leaving them behind sent pangs of guilt through her. How could she step away from the profound connections she had built with these incredible women? It was a balancing act—her love for family clashing with her commitment to those in need. Lora often found herself daydreaming about the joy of having her grandchildren nearby, their laughter filling her home, yet she couldn't shake the feeling that her purpose was here, at least for now.

Lora peered out the kitchen window, her heart swelling with warmth as she watched the renovated barn come to life. It hummed with an inviting energy, radiating a sense of sanctuary that beckoned those in need. Sunlight streamed through the stained-glass windows, casting kaleidoscopic patterns across the polished wooden floor, creating a lively dance of colors that seemed to echo the laughter and shared stories within.

This wasn't just a barn; it was a refuge, a carefully crafted haven where women could find solace and support. Each detail reflected Lora's love and dedication—the rough-hewn beams, once daunting and cold, now softened by the warm glow of the stained glass, complemented by the comforting textures of hand-stitched quilts draped over well-worn chairs. It was a space that wrapped around you like a warm hug, inviting all who entered to shed their burdens and breathe a little easier.

As Lora prepared to join the women arriving for their gathering, she felt a sense of excitement flutter within her. Each of them brought a unique story, a tapestry woven from trials and triumphs. There was Alina, a young mother wrestling with the waves of postpartum depression, her weary eyes reflecting the weight of new motherhood and the shadows of a husband lost to his drinking. Then came Martha, a vibrant grandmother whose heart still echoed with the laughter of her late husband, even as grief etched lines of loss upon her face. And there was Katrina, the brave young woman who had fought her way out of an abusive relationship, her spirit determined and fierce.

Each woman carried her own struggles, but within this shared space, they found something powerful—a sense of community that transcended their individual pain. Lora felt a surge of purpose as she stepped outside, ready to foster connections that could help heal their wounds. This barn was more than walls and windows; it was a place where isolation melted away, where hearts could open and stories could intertwine, reminding each woman that they were never alone in their journey.

Her mind wandered to Destiny, her closest friend, and all the relentless attempts she had made to pull her back from the edge of despair. The colors of life had dulled for Lora ever since that tragic day when Dawson was taken from her.

Her gaze fell on the canvas propped up in the corner of the dining room, now an art studio filled with memories and echoes of laughter. It was a painting, unfinished and longing for completion—a breathtaking scene of the lake just a stone's throw from her back door. Twenty years ago, it was this very lake that had drawn her and Dawson here, a shimmering promise of joy and adventure.

Those sun-drenched days spent fishing, swimming, and walking the trail they had built together felt like a different lifetime now. Each ripple of the water whispered stories of their happy moments, yet the sight of it pierced her heart, reminding her of the void left behind. Lora knew she needed to reclaim her art, to breathe life back into her brushstrokes, and perhaps, in doing so, to find a fragment of her spirit again.

That fateful day marked a turning point in Lora's life—a moment when everything she cherished was turned upside down. Losing the love of her life, Dawson, in that gruesome accident felt like her very heart had stopped beating alongside his. Thirty precious years they had shared, their memories now reduced to whispers of a life once vibrant, now painfully still.

Once a vibrant artist, Lora had poured herself into her paintings, each stroke a reflection of her dreams and joys. But now, those colors lay muted, and with a heavy heart, she closed the doors of her once-thriving art studio, a sanctuary where she had nurtured creativity in others. Teaching had been her passion, sharing her love for art with those eager to express themselves. But in the wake of her loss, she found herself struggling to understand how to live without Dawson's laughter and support.

Yet amidst the darkness, she clung to one thread of hope: journaling. Each day, she opened her notebook, pouring out her heart onto the pages, finding solace in the act of writing. It was a gentle reminder that while Dawson was gone, her story continued.

But her tie to the outside world was mostly the Women's Ministry she and Dawson had founded in the weathered embrace of an old barn. It had been a safe haven for women to gather, share their stories, and heal together. Even in this grief-stricken time, Lora found solace in nurturing that space, guiding others as they navigated their own heartaches. The barn, filled with laughter and tears, became a testament to resilience, a beacon of hope amidst the shadows of her own despair.

As Lora embarked on this painful journey of rediscovery, each day presented a new challenge. Yet, within the pages of her journal and the walls of the barn, she started to see glimpses of hope—small but significant reminders that life, while forever changed, held the potential for beauty once again.

Taking a deep breath, Lora made her way to the barn where the other women were gathering. The morning sun was already warm, shining down on her. Later in the evening, she'd have time to spend with her thoughts of Dawson and the impact of his loss, but for now, duty called; these women needed her, and she needed them

She knew she had to find a way beyond this emptiness she felt. It wasn't going to be easy—she knew that all too well. The past two years had been a relentless battle against her own pain, a struggle to rediscover the joy in life and to truly live again. But she had to try, if not for herself, then for her son and grandchildren. They deserved the best version of her, a grandmother who radiated warmth and love, not one weighed down by sorrow. With each step forward, Lora felt a flicker of hope ignite within her, reminding her that recovery was possible, and that she wasn't alone in this fight.

But tonight, after the tasks were done, she knew too well that she'd let herself dwell on her memories of him—the sound of his laughter, the way he'd look at her with a mixture of love and mischief. She pushed the thought aside, forcing a smile as she greeted the faces before her. This was her sanctuary—a place where laughter filled the air and warmth enveloped her. Yet, beneath the bright facade, she wrestled with the shadows of her own pain, striving to keep the turmoil hidden. With each friendly exchange, she reminded herself that she was more than her struggles; she was a tapestry of joy and sorrow woven together, longing for connection while battling the haunting echoes of her own heart.

CHAPTER 2

That afternoon, the aroma of dark roast enveloped the air like a comforting blanket against the crisp autumn chill. Rain pattered softly against the large windowpanes of The Cozy Corner, a quaint coffee shop nestled in the heart of town, where soft music hummed in the background and baristas buzzed with cheerful energy. Lora, typically content in the quiet solitude of her renovated barn, craved a change of scenery that afternoon—a brief escape from the emotional weight she carried. The coffee shop beckoned, promising warmth and distraction, even if just for a cup of coffee and a few stolen moments of peace.

Settling into a plush armchair by the window, she allowed the rhythmic patter of the rain to soothe her thoughts. On the small table beside her lay her well-worn Bible, open to a cherished passage—a symbol of her steadfast reliance on faith during this trying chapter of her life. Her fingers traced the frayed edges as she sought comfort in the familiar words, attempting to anchor herself amid the storm of emotions swirling within her.

Suddenly, a burst of laughter erupted near the counter, shattering her quiet reverie. A man—tall and broad-shouldered, radiating warmth—engaged in a jovial conversation with the barista. His laughter was rich and deep, a sound that cut through the café's gentle hum, drawing Lora's eyes to him like a moth to a flame. He had an approachable kindness about him, a presence that seemed to light up the entire room.

Their eyes met, and Lora's heart skipped a beat, a jolt of unexpected electricity coursing through her. His eyes, the color of warm honey and framed by thick, dark lashes, held a gentle intelligence and a quiet strength that resonated with her, though expressed in a completely different way. He caught her gaze and lingered just a moment longer than what politeness dictated—a silent acknowledgment that felt like a spark igniting in the air between them. A subtle charge hummed around them, transforming the atmosphere, and when he offered a small, almost imperceptible nod, it was as if the world around them had faded away.

As he turned back to the barista, the impression he left lingered—an undeniable tremor in the calmness of her afternoon. Lora fought to refocus on her Bible, but the words danced and blurred, the soothing message escaping her grasp like a wisp of smoke. Sipping her coffee, she felt its warmth travel through her, but it did little to soothe the unexpected ripple he had created in her structured routine. It wasn't just his physical presence—it was a kind of quiet magnetism, that hinted at a connection that was both unexpected and unsettling.

As he eventually made his exit, his departure was as subtle as his entrance had been, yet Lora found herself unable to shake the feeling of his presence. She couldn't remember what he ordered or the specifics of their shared glance, yet she replayed the moment in her mind, captivated by the fleeting connection. His image lingered like a beautiful melody in the back of her thoughts, an enigma that had slipped into her carefully crafted solitude. In that unexpected moment, he had become a delightful disturbance, awakening a longing for something more amidst the stillness of her life.

Later, as she stepped back into the comforting embrace of her home, Lora settled into her cozy office, journal in hand, ready for her evening ritual. Yet tonight held an unusual air, charged with an energy that set her heart racing. Instead of pouring her feelings onto the pages about Dawson—his absence still a gaping void in her life—she found herself fixated on a stranger from the coffee shop. His gaze, innocent yet piercing, had stirred something within her, a confusing blend of intrigue and longing.

Her pen danced over the paper, attempting to untangle the web of emotions that his fleeting glance had sparked. The words flowed freely at first, but as she delved deeper, she found herself lost in thoughts of possibilities—a world where sorrow mingled with hope, where grief could evolve into something unexpected.

Just as she began to lose herself in the exploration of this unexpected distraction, the cheerful chime of her doorbell pulled her back to reality. Closing her journal with a soft sigh, she tucked it away, a secret still bubbling beneath the surface. She opened the door to find her best friend, Destiny, standing there with a bright smile that instantly warmed her heart.

"Hey, beautiful! I've missed you!" Destiny exclaimed, her vibrant energy filling the room. Lora couldn't help but smile back, grateful for the interruption and the comfort of friendship. Yet, as they embraced, the question lingered in Lora's mind—had she really left the mysterious man behind, or was he about to step into her life in unexpected ways?

Lora sat on the edge of her seat, her heart racing as she weighed the decision of whether to share her new emotions with Destiny. It felt like a personal betrayal to Dawson, who had been gone for two long years. The warmth she felt earlier that day—a spark ignited by a stranger whose name she didn't even know—swirled in her heart like a wild storm. She glanced at Destiny, whose perceptive eyes were examining her with an intensity that made Lora's heart race.

Destiny sat across from her with a questioning look. "Is everything okay?" she asked, her voice tinged with concern. "You seem a little... different today."

Lora resisted the urge to roll her eyes. After years of friendship, Destiny could see right through her facade. "What do you mean—different?" she asked, forcing a casual tone that didn't quite reach her eyes. She focused on her friend's expectant gaze, knowing that if she hesitated too long, Destiny would pry deeper, uncovering feelings Lora wasn't quite ready to confront.

The moment hung in the air, charged with unspoken truths and the fear of revealing too much. Lora took a breath, battling her impulse to confide. Would sharing her muddled feelings about a stranger betray the memory of Dawson, or could it be the first step toward healing?

"Really, Destiny," Lora finally confessed, her eyes sparkling with excitement. "The only thing I did differently today was visit The Cozy Corner to read my Bible and enjoy a warm cup of coffee in a new setting away from home."

Her friend leaned in, a playful grin spreading across her face. "Well, that must have been some amazing coffee! I haven't seen you with that much color in your cheeks in ages," she teased, raising an eyebrow.

Lora chuckled, brushing a stray hair behind her ear. "And let's be real—you can't pin this on the sunlight—what sunshine? It rained all day!" Destiny swatted her knee playfully.

"What if I told you that..." Lora crinkled her forehead in thought, "Nothing really happened, but..." She paused, her mind racing to find the right words.

"But what?" Destiny leaned in, her anticipation bubbling over. "You can't start a story like that and then leave me hanging!"

"I really don't know." Lora finally smiled, an amused spark in her eyes. "There was this man who came in to get coffee." She could still feel the spark he ignited within her, even if she couldn't fully grasp it.

Destiny shot up from her seat, practically bouncing with excitement. "You met someone!" She didn't give Lora a moment to gather her thoughts before bombarding her with questions. "What's his name? What's he like? Is he from around here?" Lora chuckled, the warmth of her friend's enthusiasm easing her earlier confusion. "I don't know, I don't know, and I don't know."

Destiny's expression twisted from excitement to confusion. "Well, didn't you ask him?"

"We didn't exactly speak to each other," Lora admitted sheepishly, feeling the blush creep up her cheeks. "It was just this lingering shared glance, and then he smiled at me."

Destiny's eyes widened, sparkling with disbelief and a hint of frustration. "Oh, come on, Lora!" she exclaimed. "You felt a connection, and you let him walk out without even getting his name? That's like letting a rare comet pass by without wishing on it!"

Lora laughed, an electric thrill coursing through her. "Okay, I admit, it was a little... magical? But what could I say? 'Hi, I'm Lora, and I'm completely entranced by this single moment?'"

"Yes! Exactly!" Destiny clapped her hands together, her excitement infectious. "You have to seize the moment! What if he's 'the one'? You can't let an opportunity like this slip away!"

A smile blossomed on Lora's face, fueled by the exciting rush of possibility. "Or what if he's just another stranger in the coffee shop?" she thought, a pang of uncertainty creeping in. Suddenly, a more unsettling idea surfaced: "What if he doesn't feel the same way? What if that spark I sensed was just a figment of my imagination? He could have simply been being polite."

"Then you at least have the best story for your next coffee run," Destiny shot back with a grin. "Besides, who knows? If God meant for you to connect, maybe you'll run into him again!"

The thought sent a rush of butterflies through Lora's stomach—what if she did see him again? "Maybe I should start hanging out at that coffee shop more often, just in case!"

"Yes! And don't forget to practice your smooth introduction!" Destiny teased, both of them giggling as they let the idea of chance romance linger in the air.

Leaning into her, Destiny had a radiant glow, her eyes sparkling with conviction. "Lora..." Destiny began, her voice steady. "It's time for you to embrace a new chapter. You're not dishonoring Dawson's memory; you're honoring it by living fully. He would've wanted you to find happiness again."

The sincerity in Destiny's tone struck a chord within Lora, stirring emotions she had buried for too long. A soft wave of reassurance washed over her, leaving her wondering if perhaps it truly was time to take that leap. The thought of Dawson wanting her to find love again ignited a flicker of hope, making the future seem a little less daunting and a lot more inviting. Now, if only God would allow a second chance meeting.

As the door clicked softly behind Destiny, Lora couldn't help but smile, her heart warming at her friend's excitement. Destiny's joy over the prospect of Lora finding someone new was infectious. Lora had initially worried that Destiny might think she was moving too fast, but she couldn't have been more mistaken.

CHAPTER 3

In the days that followed, Lora found herself in an unexpected game of hide and seek, her heart racing as she searched for the mysterious man who had captured her imagination. She scoured the grocery market, scrutinized the aisles of the pharmacy, and indulged her sweet tooth at the bakery, all in the hopes of catching a glimpse of him again. The Cozy Corner became her second home, each visit fueled by the hope that she might find him seated at one of its cozy booths, sharing a laugh with the barista.

But after days of searching, she began to doubt if he was even real; perhaps the man she had seen was simply a figment of her imagination, a fleeting wisp of a dream. Just when she was about to give up, fortune smiled upon her. As she pulled up to Ben's Garage on Main Street, there he was—stepping into the gray truck that had always seemed like a ghost in her mind. Her heart raced as he climbed into his vehicle, a perfect flannel shirt hugging his frame as he waved goodbye to Ben. Without a second thought, she sat frozen in her car, the bell chiming as she arrived at the pump, an ironic reminder of her arrival—and presence.

"Fill it up," she said with a nervous smile, her eyes still glued to the direction he had just taken. Ben chuckled, the familiar sound oddly comforting, as he moved to fill her tank. Lora's mind churned with possibilities—who was he, this enigma that stirred something deep within her?

As Ben handed her the receipt, she gathered her courage. "Hey, Ben," she ventured, trying to sound casual, "do you happen to know who that guy was—the one who just left?"

With a quizzical look, Ben racked his brain before offering, "Ah, can't say I know his name, but he's a regular here. Works for Brooks Construction. He's in here all the time getting gas and oil for the equipment."

Her pulse quickened. Brooks Construction was local, a sign he was new to town and had roots just starting to grow. Hope bloomed in Lora's chest as she contemplated the possibilities—a chance encounter, a spark waiting to ignite.

As she pulled away from Ben's Garage, Lora couldn't shake the conversation she'd just had. It was interesting that the man she'd been daydreaming about was a regular there. But how many more excuses could she conjure up to visit Ben's? She chuckled at the idea—what would Ben think of her sudden, frequent stops? Would he see right through her little charade?

At fifty, Lora felt like a giddy teenager, besotted and a bit ridiculous. What would Destiny say if she knew Lora was on the hunt for this mysterious man? Destiny would undoubtedly have a field day, teasing her mercilessly. But Lora couldn't help it; something about him stirred a spark she hadn't felt in ages. After all, she had married Dawson straight out of high school, and in their thirty years together, no other man had managed to ignite even the faintest flicker of excitement in her.

Once she was back home to her cozy cottage, Lora sank into her favorite Adirondack chair on the back deck, cradling a warm cup of Genmaicha tea between her hands. The soothing aroma of roasted rice filled the air as she gazed out at the charming old barn, its stained-glass windows shimmering in the afternoon sun. Memories flooded her mind, reminding her of the divine spark that ignited her journey to start the women's ministry.

In those early days, the meetings took place in her living room, but with Ethan entering his teenage years, the house had turned into a whirlwind of energy, filled with a constant stream of teenage boys. A sense of chaos had settled in, making it nearly impossible to find a moment of quiet. That's when Dawson stepped in with a brilliant suggestion: why not transform the old barn into a gathering space?

At first, they spent a whole year merely cleaning it out, uncovering forgotten treasures and dusting off decades of memories. But just when Lora thought their dream might remain just that—a dream—Dawson surprised her one day with Brooks Construction pulling up to begin renovations. With each plank laid and every window restored, the barn slowly evolved into the vibrant community hub it is today, a testament to faith, friendship, and the power of a shared vision.

Suddenly, a realization struck her like a bolt of lightning—
Ian at Brooks Construction! Memories flooded back; Ian
Brooks had always been more than just a businessman to
Dawson—they were practically family. Their bond
stretched back to when Ian's family first relocated from
bustling Chicago to this quaint little town.

Eager to establish his construction business, he stepped into
Dawson's office to fill out a business application. Their
conversation had revealed a surprising number of shared
interests despite the age gap, and before long, the new
arrival had become a familiar face. He spent countless
afternoons fishing with Dawson and Ethan, casting their
lines into the shimmering lake, their laughter echoing off the
water.

Now, thinking about it, Ian would definitely know who the
charming mystery man was that she had spotted at The Cozy
Corner. Ben had mentioned he worked for Brooks
Construction—what were the odds?

A mischievous smile crept across Lora's face as she
imagined broaching the topic with Ian. "Hey Ian," she
chuckled to herself, "there's this incredibly handsome guy
with the most captivating amber-honey eyes working for
you, and he's around my age—who is he?" Just as she
entertained the thought, the melodious chime of the doorbell
cut through her reverie, pulling her back to reality. Who
could that be?

As Lora swung open the front door, she was greeted by the
cheerful sight of Martha, standing there with a plate

wrapped in shiny foil. "Martha!" Lora exclaimed, her eyes lighting up. "It's a delight to see you! Come in!"

Martha's eyes sparkled as she extended the plate, her smile radiating kindness. "I hope I'm not intruding, but I baked an apple pie," she said cheerfully. "I can't manage a whole pie by myself, so I thought I'd share some sweetness with you."

Lora's heart warmed at the gesture as she accepted the plate, the sweet aroma wafting into her nose. "Oh, what a delight! I always adore your pies--and your cakes!" she gushed, motioning for Martha to take a seat at the cozy kitchen table, where sunlight danced on the surface.

Martha chuckled softly, shaking her head. "Oh, no, dear, I must be getting back. My son is coming by later, and I promised I'd have dinner ready for him." Her warm smile never faltered, leaving a lingering glow in the room.

As Lora began to unwrap the foil, the promise of a delicious slice of pie hung in the air, and she couldn't help but feel that this unexpected visit was the sweetest part of her day. As she placed the shiny foil back over her homemade pie, she walked Martha to the door, feeling the warmth of their conversation lingering in the air.

Just as the older woman reached for the doorknob, Lora couldn't help herself and blurted out, "Martha..." The words came tumbling out before she could think twice, "Is Ian still active at Brooks Construction—or has he retired already?" The thought of Ian's age struck her, a quiet realization dawning that he and Martha were both in that delicate chapter of life.

Martha's expression shifted, sadness washing over her like a gentle wave. "Oh, no, dear," she said softly. "Ian Brooks passed away about six months ago." The weight of the news settled heavily in the air between them. "I'm not sure who's in charge over there now." Just as she turned to leave, Martha hesitated, glancing back with a knowing look. "Why? Do you have something that needs to be done?"

"Oh, no," Lora felt a blush creep to her cheeks, as if she'd been caught harboring secrets. "I was just sitting out on the back deck admiring the work he did on the old barn and happened to be thinking about him."

Martha's expression softened, a warm smile gracing her lips. "He sure loved to fish here in the lake out back. Such a good man…" Her voice trailed off, nostalgia evident in her eyes. With that, she climbed into her car, the gentle hum of the engine echoing the bittersweet memory of a kind soul.

Lora couldn't help but smile as she watched Martha navigate her way out of the driveway, marveling at the woman's spirit. For someone nearing her eighties, she was undeniably feisty, full of life, and brimming with stories. Lora took a deep breath; She was completely unaware of Ian's passing; her heart was still heavy with the loss of Dawson, consuming her thoughts and emotions.

Just as Lora returned to the tantalizing apple pie sitting on the counter, the doorbell chimed again. She turned with a playful lilt in her voice. "Did you forget...something?" she teased, only to freeze in surprise as she opened the door to reveal Destiny, holding two steaming cups of coffee from The Cozy Corner.

"What?" Destiny grinned, lifting the cups with mock seriousness. "Is coffee not enough?"

Lora's eyes sparkled with excitement. "You won't believe it! Martha just dropped by with her famous homemade apple pie!" Her smile broadened as the sweet scent wafted through the air.

At the mention of the pie, Destiny's eyes lit up. "Oh, you're kidding me!" Without waiting for an invitation, she dashed toward the kitchen, her excitement palpable. "I am totally inviting myself to have some!"

After devouring generous slices of pie, Lora beckoned her friend Destiny to join her on the back deck. The sun was dipping low in the sky, painting everything in hues of orange and gold while a crisp autumn chill settled around them. Lora gathered a few logs and tossed them into the firepit, the flames crackling to life and enveloping them in comforting warmth as they settled in for a chat.

"Did you hear that Ian Brooks passed away?" Lora asked, a hint of concern in her voice.

Destiny's expression softened as she met Lora's gaze. "Yeah, it's been... about six months now," she replied, her tone heavy with empathy. Lora felt the silence stretch between them, thick with unspoken words. She knew that look well; it was the one everyone wore when they recalled the shadow of Dawson's loss.

"I saw him today," Lora blurted out, trying to shift the mood.

Destiny's brow furrowed in horrified confusion. "You saw who—Ian Brooks?"

"No!" Lora chuckled, shaking her head. "That would be weird—seeing as he's dead."

"Thank goodness!" Destiny rolled her eyes, a playful smile breaking through the tension. "For a second there, I thought you had truly lost it and were ready for the looney farm!" She chuckled before leaning in closer, curiosity sparkling in her eyes. "So... who did you see?"

Lora's playful smile widened. "The guy from The Cozy Corner!"

Destiny perked up, her legs crossed in excitement as she leaned forward. "And... did you talk to him?"

Lora shook her head, but before she could explain, Destiny jumped in. "What? Lora! Why not?" she exclaimed, hands flying up in that dramatic flair only her friend could pull off. "You can't keep doing this!"

"Okay, okay, let me finish!" Lora laughed, finding her friend's theatrics amusing. "He was just pulling out of Ben's as I was pulling in, so I couldn't exactly chat with him." She playfully swatted at Destiny. "But I did ask Ben about him!"

"Oooh, look at you, being all sneaky," Destiny teased, leaning forward, her curiosity piqued. "What did Ben say?"

Lora settled back into her seat, letting out a huff of air. "Not much, just that he works with Brooks Construction," she replied, her expression shifting to one of contemplation. "That's when Ian popped into my mind. I thought about reaching out, you know, to see if he could shed some light on things. But then I asked Martha if Ian was still with

Brooks Construction—and that's when she revealed he passed away six months ago."

Destiny gazed at the stars as if each twinkle held the potential solutions. "Why not reach out to Brooks Construction?" she suggested earnestly, her voice laced with seriousness that unsettled Lora.

"No way!" Lora let out a nervous chuckle, her eyes wide with uncertainty. "I could have found a way to reach out to Ian—I know him well enough. But a complete stranger? What would I even say?" She sat up, her expression shifting to a mix of determination and embarrassment. "Do you happen to know if there's a guy around 50 who works there? You know, salt and pepper hair, those mesmerizing amber-honey eyes? What would I say then? Those eyes electrified me, and I just have to find him?"

The two erupted into laughter, the absurdity of the situation a welcome distraction. Destiny playfully nudged her friend, "But think about it! You might discover something new—at worst, you might scare him off! But hey, at least you'd know more than you do now."

They continued to giggle, imagining all the ridiculous scenarios that could unfold from a simple phone call. Both knew it was a silly idea, but in that bubble of shared excitement, anything felt possible.

As the door closed behind Destiny, Lora found herself enveloped in a haze of thoughts, swirling like the autumn leaves caught in a gentle breeze outside. Who was this mystery man who had stirred something deep within her?

The weight of his mysterious presence lingered in her mind, igniting a curiosity she hadn't felt in years.

Her thoughts drifted to Dawson—the love they had built over three decades was solid, unwavering. Yet, as she reminisced, an unsettling realization washed over her. Their bond, though filled with warmth and shared memories, had never sparked the kind of electric connection she had felt with a complete stranger. It wasn't that Dawson hadn't been everything she needed; it was just—different.

Could it be that youth had obscured her recognition of true passion? Or was this newfound spark simply a fleeting emotion, a trick of fate momentarily diverting her heart? The guilt tugged at her heart as she grappled with the intoxicating thrill this unknown man ignited within her—an excitement she had never experienced with the one she had shared her life with.

And yet, when she thought of the stranger's eyes—those captivating pools of mystery—Lora felt drawn to the unknown like a moth to a flame. There was something inexplicable about him, something that clutched at her core and begged to be explored. The pull was irresistible, and deep down, she knew she had to uncover the truth about who he was. What was it about him that captivated her so thoroughly?

Determined to chase this feeling rather than run from it, Lora set her mind on a path toward discovery. After all, life was too brief to ignore the whispers of the heart, even when they led her into uncharted territory. With a heart pounding with both excitement and trepidation, she resolved to find out more about this man who had ignited a fire she thought had long been extinguished. Could God be giving her a second chance at love?

As Lora made her way to bed, her mind buzzed with thoughts of him. She couldn't shake the feeling that fate had played a role in their brief encounter. With a hopeful heart, she whispered a heartfelt prayer: "God, if there's something you're trying to reveal about this man, if he's meant to be a part of my life, please let our paths cross again."

Feeling a sense of calm wash over her, she climbed into bed, the soft rustle of her sheets a comforting embrace. She switched off the lamp beside her, plunging the room into a gentle darkness, but it was illuminated with the warmth of possibility. As sleep began to beckon her, she allowed herself to dream of chance encounters and the magic of what could be.

CHAPTER 4

At the women's ministry meetings, held on Tuesdays and Thursdays, the atmosphere is usually a blend of familiar faces and heartfelt discussions. This past Tuesday was no different, but as the doors opened on Thursday, Lora was greeted by a wave of new participants. Among them was a woman who caught Lora's attention—she seemed lost in her thoughts, grappling with a profound dilemma.

Her struggle was palpable as she shared how difficult it was to accept that her mom was dating someone new, just two years after her dad's passing. Lora felt a knot form in her stomach; the weight of the woman's pain resonated deeply within her.

It struck her like a lightning bolt: What about Ethan? Her son. Had she ever stopped to consider how her own quest for companionship might affect him? While she contemplated the idea of meeting a stranger she'd barely even known, a sudden wave of doubt washed over her. Would Ethan be okay with her pursuing a new relationship?

As the discussion continued, Lora's heart raced. The idea of tracking down that mysterious man from the coffee shop now felt like an emotional tightrope walk. Would her son see her as moving on, or would he feel left behind? The complexity of love and loss wrapped around her thoughts, compelling her to seek not just her happiness but to ensure Ethan's feelings were part of the journey.

In that moment, Lora felt a wave of clarity wash over her. Love, she realized, was no longer just about fluttering heartbeats and electric connections. It was about something deeper—understanding and compassion, both for herself and for her son. Sure, he was a grown man now, happily building his own life out in Texas, miles away from her. Yet, a stirring in her heart urged her to reach out, to connect, to get his thoughts on her venturing into the world of dating again.

It wasn't that she wanted his approval—far from it—but something about the idea of re-entering the romantic sphere made her feel both excited and nervous. Would he be happy for her? Would he worry? She could already picture his face, scrunching up in that adorable way he did when he thought she was being too adventurous.

With a deep breath and a flicker of a smile, she sat in front of her computer and checked if he was available for FaceTime. Of course, she wouldn't dive into the details of the charming mystery man in the coffee shop just yet; that would be a surprise for another day. For now, she simply wanted to hear her son's voice, to feel connected, to share this new chapter of her life with someone who mattered deeply to her.

Within mere seconds, the familiar and handsome face of her son flickered to life on the screen before Lora. She couldn't help but smile, her heart swelling at the sight of him. "Hi, Mom," Ethan greeted her, but his eyes were clouded with concern. "Is everything okay?"

This wasn't their usual time to chat—she typically waited for the weekends when he and Ava had a moment to breathe. "Oh, yes," she replied, forcing a smile, "I just felt the urge to talk to my son." Yet, despite her bright exterior, she hesitated, trying to find the right words to tackle the topic weighing on her mind.

"Okay…" Ethan's voice lingered, and Lora could see him trying to read her. "Something's up; I can hear it in your tone."

He knew her so well. This was going to be more challenging than she'd anticipated. "I want to talk to you about something," Lora started, her heart racing. "I need to know how you would feel about… something." She stumbled over her words, the nerves creeping in and choking her resolve.

"What's really up, Mom?" His expression shifted to worry. "You're not acting like yourself."

"Nothing… really… I'm fine," she stammered, forcing a tender smile at him through the screen. Then, taking a deep breath, she let it spill out. "What would you do if I found someone?"

Ethan's eyes widened, sparkling with excitement. "You met someone!" he exclaimed, his tone bouncing with enthusiasm. "Mom, that is awesome! Who is he? Do I know him?" His questions tumbled out in rapid succession.

"No, no, no!" Lora giggled, a mix of shock and laughter bubbling up. "I only want to know how you would feel if I did."

"Oh," he said, his face suddenly serious as it dropped. "You should. Honestly, I'd feel better if you had someone, especially with me being so far away."

Relief washed over her as she sat on the edge of her chair, digging deeper. "So you wouldn't be upset?" she prompted. "Or think it's too soon?"

Ethan leaned forward, his expression softening. "Mom, it's been two years since we lost Dad." His voice was steady and full of warmth. "It's past time for you to move on—Dad would have wanted it that way."

In that moment, Lora felt a blend of emotions: hope, fear, and an unexpected sense of freedom. Maybe it was time to open her heart again. As the call wrapped up, Lora smiled, sending a warm message to Ethan: "Please give my love to Ava and the kids. I can't wait to catch up with them on Saturday!"

Sitting in the soft glow of her screen, she couldn't shake the excitement she felt. Ethan's face had lit up with joy at the mere thought of her moving on, and that thrill sent a rush of hope through her. It felt like a weight had lifted—she wouldn't have to worry about him feeling like that woman in the meeting today, lost and unsure.

His words echoed in her mind: Dawson would have wanted her to find happiness. That thought alone was both soothing and invigorating. Lora knew that embracing the future could be daunting, but she was determined to honor Dawson's memory by welcoming joy back into her life.

As she stepped into her kitchen, the memory of that fateful night washed over her like a tidal wave, pulling her back into a past she had hoped to forget. Lora decided to brew herself a strong cup of coffee—tonight, she needed something with a kick to navigate her journey down memory lane.

With her favorite sherpa blanket draped over her arm, she made her way to the back deck, her sanctuary. It was the perfect spot, offering an unobstructed view of the sprawling backyard, the glimmering lake, and the charmingly renovated barn that stood proudly in the distance. As the sun began its descent, painting the sky with hues of orange and pink, she settled into her favorite chair, enveloped in warmth and nostalgia.

The tranquility of the scene contrasted sharply with the whirlwind of thoughts in her mind. The gentle rustle of leaves and the soft lapping of water at the shore seemed to whisper secrets of the past, inviting her to confront the emotions she had buried deep within. This trip down memory lane might be the key to understanding the choices that led her here, and she felt a shiver of anticipation mixed with trepidation as she cradled her steaming cup—a companion for the reflections to come.

That week had flown by in a whirlwind of laughter and cherished moments. Megan, now two months old, had quickly captured the hearts of her family. Ethan and Ava felt it was the perfect opportunity for a family adventure, packing to travel with the tiny bundle along with her spirited three-year-old twin brothers, Aiden and Noah.

Dawson, the ever-proud papa, relished every moment spent fishing with Ethan and the grandsons by the shimmering lake. The sound of their laughter echoed through the trees, mingling with the gentle lapping of water against the shore. Meanwhile, Lora enjoyed serene afternoons on the deck, tea in hand and the sun warming her face, as she marveled at the sweetness of baby Megan nestled in her arms.

As Saturday morning dawned, the joy of their Georgia getaway mingled with a hint of sadness. It was time to head back home to Texas after a week steeped in love and connection. Dawson, always the doting father, had eagerly volunteered to drive them to the Atlanta airport, an hour and a half trek that he deemed more worthwhile than a taxi ride. This was a chance for one last flood of memories before they parted ways.

Lora chose to stay behind, believing her absence would provide more space for the car ride. She walked the others to the door, her heart swelling with affection as she kissed each one goodbye. When it came to Dawson, their lingering farewell was imbued with a warmth that made her smile, not knowing it would be the last. As he turned to drive away, he shot her a playful wink that sent a jolt of love through her. Little did she know, that delightful image of him, full of life and laughter, would be a bittersweet memory forever etched in her mind—a haunting reminder of their last moments together, moments that would soon become all too precious.

Before they departed, Dawson had promised Lora he would be back home by noon. The day had other plans, though— airport delays and traffic jams turned that promise into a waiting game. But all day, he kept her in the loop, calling and texting, reassuring her that he was on his way. By 2 PM, Ethan rang her up, his voice a mix of relief and excitement as he shared that he and his family had finally made it home.

Lora couldn't help but smile through her anxiety as she explained to Ethan that his dad was stuck in traffic but was close. Just after she hung up with Ethan, Dawson's voice filled her ear—he was only twenty minutes away. Relief washed over her, but a slight unease lingered as the clock ticked.

But then, at 5 PM, the doorbell rang, shattering the fragile peace in her heart. A wave of dread rolled over her like a dark cloud before she even opened the door. Standing there was a state trooper, his face grim and serious. The moment she saw his uniform, icy dread gripped her heart.

"Do you know a Dawson Bennett?" he asked gently, and Lora's numb nod spoke volumes.

"There's been an accident out on HWY 52," he continued, his voice soft yet firm. He paused, compassion etched on his face. "Do you have a way to the hospital here in town?"

Her heart raced as panic surged within her. "Is he okay— please, tell me he's okay," she pleaded, voice trembling, as if grasping for a lifeline in a stormy sea of dread.

"Ma'am, if you don't have transportation, I can take you," he offered, his eyes avoiding hers, but the unspoken truth hung heavily in the air. That's when Lora felt it: a crushing realization that shattered her world—Dawson, the love of her life, was gone.

The next few hours felt like a jagged dream, memories blurring together in a haze of disbelief. As they sped towards the hospital, she dialed Ethan's number, her heart pounding. The words tumbled out, heavy with dread. "It's bad, Ethan. I don't know everything yet, but…"

"Is he alive?" Ethan's voice cracked, panic electrifying the air between them. "Mom! Is he alive?" The urgency in his tone sent a fresh wave of despair rolling through her. She could hear Ava in the background, her small voice whispering questions that cut through the tension.

"They haven't said… they're avoiding answering me directly," Lora replied, shooting a glance at the silent officer driving her. The quiet urgency in the car only fueled her anxiety. "Destiny and Frank are meeting me there. I'll call when I know more." The call ended with a dread that hung heavy in the air.

As they arrived at the hospital, Lora stepped out of the car, adrenaline surging. Destiny came barreling towards her, eyes wide with terror. "Where is he?" Lora's voice broke, desperation clawing at her throat. "Where is Dawson?"

In that moment, Lora's worst fear crystallized as Destiny pulled her into a tight embrace, her own tears mingling with Lora's. "Lora! No, please!" Destiny's voice cracked as she held her friend, the weight of their loss hanging heavy in the air. "He's gone... and you don't want to see him like this."

But Lora's grief surged like a tidal wave, crashing over her. "I want to go to my husband now!" she affirmed, her voice a fierce whisper, laced with pain. "Destiny—Frank," she urged, her eyes pleading for understanding. "Take me to him... please."

Seeing the determination in her eyes, Destiny and Frank exchanged a glance, knowing there was no way to stop her. They led her inside, and a nurse guided them to the room where Dawson lay. The world around her faded as the door swung open, and Lora's breath caught in her throat. The man she knew and loved was unrecognizable, his handsome features obscured by the harsh reality of what had happened.

In that moment, a rush of regret overwhelmed her. If only she had listened to Destiny and Frank, she could have spared herself from this heartbreak, from this final, gut-wrenching image of him.

In the hallway, a trooper—a different one now—approached with the weight of a tragic story in his eyes. "A semi-truck ran around the curve on the wrong side of the road," he explained softly. "Dawson had nowhere to go, no time to react... just 15 minutes from home."

In that instant, Lora's world shattered. She stood frozen in the face of unbearable loss, grappling with the reality of a future without Dawson—a future she had no idea how to navigate. The grief enveloped her, and in that moment, she was irrevocably changed, left wondering how she would ever learn to live in the hollow space where her husband once stood.

As she stepped into the house, Lora wiped her tears, as if wiping away the ache of that terrible night. Her gaze fell on the picture of Dawson, his warm smile radiating from the kitchen counter. She picked it up gently, her heart swelling with emotion. "It's been two years since the night you left, and I still love you with all my heart and soul," she whispered softly, her voice laced with longing. "I will always cherish what we had and the memories we shared— we truly had a good life together."

Setting the picture back on the kitchen counter, Lora took a deep breath, grounding herself in the present. "But I have to believe that God is giving me a second chance," she said quietly, determination sparking in her eyes. "And I plan on grasping it with everything in me."

With newfound resolve, she made her way to her office, the comfort of her journal waiting for her. Each page was a sanctuary where she could pour out her heart, a place to reconcile her past and embrace the promise of a brighter future. It was time to turn the page and write the next chapter of her life.

CHAPTER 5

As Friday morning broke, Lora leaped from the bed, a spark of renewed energy coursing through her veins. It was as if the cool night air on the deck had worked some magic, allowing her to confront the shadows of that tragic evening. Memories that once felt like shackles now seemed lighter, almost as if they had been swept away with the dawn. With each step she took, Lora felt a sense of liberation—a chance to breathe deeply and embrace life once more. Today was a blank canvas, and she was ready to paint it with vibrant colors of hope and possibility.

Lora smiled at her reflection in the mirror, a newfound brightness lighting up her features. Today felt different—Destiny had been right; that glow, which had been missing for far too long, was finally back. She looked in disbelief, hardly recognizing the youthful woman staring back at her. At fifty, she seemed to defy time, and a spark of joy ignited within her, rekindling feelings she thought she had lost.

With a rush of optimism, she picked up her phone and scrolled to a number she hadn't dialed in two years. Taking a deep breath, she punched in the digits and waited.

"Hi, Sharon!" Lora's voice burst with enthusiasm as soon as her friend's familiar tone came through. "It's Lora—remember me?"

The old friends chatted eagerly, sharing laughter and stories that bridged the gap of lost time. It felt like no years had passed at all. By the end of their conversation, Lora had booked an appointment to rejuvenate her look with highlights and a haircut that would enhance the youthful vitality she was embracing.

To top it off, she decided to treat herself to a mani-pedi afterward—and she couldn't resist inviting Destiny along for a much-needed girls' day. After two long years, they were well overdue for a little pampering and plenty of laughter. Lora felt her heart flutter at the thought of rediscovering that cherished friendship. This day was going to be special.

As Lora stepped into her walk-in closet, a world of possibilities surrounded her. She wandered to the back, where a collection of flowy, feminine pieces awaited her touch, each one whispering stories of past adventures. Today, she felt a surge of inspiration.

After a moment of rummaging through the fabric, she spotted a stunning skirt that hugged snugly at the waist and hips, cascading down in a graceful flow to just past her calves. It was the perfect blend of elegance and comfort, ideal for the crisp autumn air. She couldn't resist the thought of pairing it with those tall boots she had bought on a whim but never had the chance to wear. The earthy colors of the skirt were a perfect match for the fall foliage outside.

Lora quickly found a fitted shirt that clung just right, accentuating her silhouette. She could already envision the final look in her mind—a blend of chic sophistication and playful charm. Energized by her outfit choice, she set out on a mission to find the perfect jewelry—something that would add just the right touch of sparkle and personality to her ensemble.

With each piece she considered, her excitement grew. Maybe a delicate necklace with a hint of gold? Or some statement earrings that danced with each movement?

Opting for simplicity with a touch of elegance, Lora chose to adorn herself with delicate gold earrings, each featuring a tiny pearl glimmering just beneath her earlobes. As she stepped back from the full-length mirror, a smile spread across her face—the reflection revealed a transformation that felt both refreshing and empowering. Satisfied with her look, she grabbed her bag and made her way to the door. The excitement bubbled within her; a hair makeover awaited, and soon, she would be off to meet Destiny to indulge in some pampering at the nail salon.

As Lora stepped into the hair salon, she felt a familiar thrill wash over her. Sharon was already there, waiting with a warm smile. Two hours spent transforming her hair had felt nothing short of refreshing, almost therapeutic. It amazed her how different this experience was compared to two years ago when dread would wash over her every time it was time for a touch-up. But today was different; today, she felt a spark of renewal, as if she were shedding an old skin.

Now, standing outside the nail salon, anticipation bubbled within her as she awaited Destiny's arrival. It was as if the world was suddenly vivid and alive, the colors brighter and the sounds sharper. While she scanned her surroundings, her heart skipped a beat—the man from The Cozy Corner! Her eyes first caught sight of the gray truck adorned with the big Brooks Construction sign. As he maneuvered out of a parking space, she focused in on him, the very essence of casual charm. He didn't see her, and she was too far away to call out, but thoughts swirled in her mind. What would she even say? "Hi, I spotted you once at The Cozy Corner and have been searching for you ever since"? The thought made her giggle, just as Destiny appeared behind her.

"Who are you talking to?" Destiny questioned, raising an eyebrow while taking in Lora's freshly styled hair and vibrant outfit. "And look at you all dressed up—absolutely stunning!" She playfully fluffed Lora's hair, which only made her blush deepen.

Lora quickly brushed aside the questions, opting to steer the conversation away. "Are you ready for some pampering?" she asked, linking arms with Destiny and pulling her toward the nail salon's entrance.

Once inside, chaos enveloped them—customers chattering, nail technicians busy with their craft. Despite the hustle and bustle, Lora felt a twinge of disappointment as they got separated in the crowd. But there was a silver lining; it offered her a quiet moment to reflect on her earlier encounter with the coffee shop man. She chuckled at the idea of having to refer to him as "the coffee shop man"— she desperately needed a name to match that striking face. And what a face it was, captivating and handsome, lingering in her thoughts like a sweet melody.

They finished their manicure at about the same time, the sound of laughter echoing as they stepped out of the nail salon. "How about we grab some lunch at Seafood Haven?" she suggested, glancing back at Destiny as they stepped onto the bustling sidewalk. The inviting glow of Seafood Haven was just two doors down, and the promise of fresh seafood felt like the perfect way to wrap up their pampering session.

Destiny shot her a teasing look, her brow raised playfully. "Sounds great, but I must admit, I feel a little underdressed next to you." She nudged Lora gently, a mischievous grin tugging at her lips.

"Please," Lora laughed, flicking her hair over her shoulder. "You always look chic! I'm the one who usually throws on whatever's clean and calls it a day!" She returned the nudge with a playful jab of her elbow.

"I just love seeing you back to your old self," Destiny said warmly, her smile softening. "It's been too long since I've seen this vibrant version of you."

As they entered Seafood Haven, they were pleasantly surprised by how quickly they were seated. The fragrant aroma of garlic and lemon wafted through the air, making their mouths water in anticipation. Once they had settled into their cozy booth and placed their orders, Lora couldn't help but glance at Destiny, a cheeky grin spreading across her face. "So, you won't believe who I saw while waiting for you outside the nail salon."

Destiny leaned in, curious. "Oh? And did you at least manage to get his name?"

"Nope!" Lora chuckled, shaking her head in mock despair. "He was too far away and headed the opposite direction. It was a lost cause!" She playfully kicked Destiny under the table, laughter dancing in her eyes.

Destiny rolled her eyes and giggled. "Why is this man so elusive? He always seems to be just out of reach?"

"Tell me about it," Lora exclaimed, letting out a heavy sigh as she settled into her chair. At that moment, Destiny began unraveling the events of the day before, disentangling a mixture of frustration and revelation. Destiny leaned in, eager for the story.

"It all started at the morning meeting," she said, her brow furrowing as she recalled the woman who, with one casual remark, had planted a seed of thought in her mind. "You wouldn't believe how one simple comment can stir up everything! Then there was my talk with Ethan. He really has a way of cutting through the noise, you know? He said something that struck me: Dawson would want me to be happy and find love again."

As she spoke, Lora felt a surprising sense of release. The biggest release had come from reliving that tragic night, it had brought with it a flood of emotions, but also an unexpected clarity. "It's like," she continued, her voice growing steadier, "I realized I had been holding onto the past, thinking I could somehow change it. But deep down, I know that's impossible. Accepting that truth was painful, yet liberating. It was that moment of facing the hurt and letting it wash over me that made me understand—I need to start living again."

Destiny nodded, captivated by Lora's journey from despair to acceptance. "That's powerful," she replied softly, sensing the shift in her friend. "It's like you're finally finding your way back to yourself."

"So," Lora said, her smile taking on a playful glint, "if nothing else comes from that spark the man in the coffee shop ignited, at least it helped me heal."

Destiny leaned in closer, her eyes sparkling with mischief. "Oh, I believe there's definitely something special happening there. Just you wait! When God knows you're ready, that man will just appear before you, as if he's been summoned by fate itself."

Lora laughed lightly, feeling a blend of excitement and curiosity. "You really think that's how it works?"

"Absolutely!" Destiny replied, a confident nod affirming her words. "Life has a way of surprising us—especially when we least expect it. Just think about how many stories start like that! You never know when that spark will turn into something incredible."

"I agree," Lora nodded, a hint of a smile playing on her lips, "but I must admit—I've truly enjoyed the chase and the mystery."

Laughter danced between them, a fleeting moment of lightness before they parted ways. As she walked home, Lora felt a strange mixture of nostalgia and determination swell within her. It was time to reclaim her space. For two long years, Dawson had lingered like a ghost in their once-shared home, the walls adorned with his pictures and mementos that had become a shrine to the life they once had.

But now, the memories felt different. She realized she didn't need to surround herself with reminders to keep him alive in her heart. Those cherished moments, the laughter, and love they had shared would forever be etched in her soul. With each step, she decided that instead of holding onto the past, she would honor Dawson by stepping into her future.

As she entered their old home, Lora took a deep breath and surveyed the familiar surroundings. It was time to let go, to transform the shrine back into a space of hope and possibility. She rolled up her sleeves, determined to create a new chapter where the warmth of memories could coexist with the promise of new beginnings.

CHAPTER 6

The following day unfolded like a canvas brushed with the warm tones of early autumn. Lora stepped into the crisp air, a flurry of vibrant leaves swirling around her ankles as she made her way into town. Her heart quickened as she approached the familiar coffee shop, a delightful rendezvous with her favorite retreat. She nestled into her usual spot by the window, sunlight streaming through like liquid gold, illuminating the cozy nook she adored.

This visit, however, held no ties to the enigmatic man with the electric gaze whose shadow still danced in her memories from their last encounter weeks ago. Instead, she laid out her treasured possessions—a well-worn Bible and a journal filled with her musings—on the table before her. As she flipped through the familiar pages, her fingers brushed against the inked words of her favorite passages, seeking solace and inspiration in their promise.

Yet, despite her attempts to immerse herself in the comfort of her reading, her thoughts kept wandering back to him— the mystery man who had captivated her so unexpectedly.

What was his name? Did he belong to someone else, or was he as single as she was? A swirl of unanswered questions formed a knot in her stomach, demanding her attention. Always one to find clarity in words, she turned back to her books, hoping to unravel the tangled web of her curiosity—perhaps a deeper truth lay just beyond the pages.

At the sound of the door swinging open, Lora stole a quick glance up from her journal. She had just lifted her steaming cup of coffee to her lips, but time seemed to freeze as she caught sight of him. There he was, stepping into the cozy coffee shop with the same effortless grace that had captured her attention weeks ago. His warm smile illuminated the room, and as their eyes locked across the bustling space, a powerful recognition flickered between them—one that felt rooted in something deeper than the brief encounter they had shared before.

He approached the counter, ordering with an easy charm that had the barista laughing. Lora quickly turned her focus back to her Bible and journal, but the air around her crackled with an undeniable energy. It took every ounce of willpower not to glance in his direction again. But this time was undeniably different. A shadow descended over her table, drawing her gaze upward, and there he was—standing just behind the chair across from her. Lora's heart raced, pounding hard against her ribcage as her eyes locked onto his, finding a shy sincerity etched across his features.

"Hi there," he began, his voice a smooth baritone that radiated warmth and an unexpected confidence. "I believe we met a couple of weeks ago. I'm Curtis Brooks."

Surprise danced in Lora's chest, mingling with an excitement she hadn't anticipated. A small smile broke free despite her earlier composure. "Lora Bennett," she replied, her voice a tad husky, revealing her blend of shock and the flutter of mixed emotions stirring inside her.

As he motioned toward the vacant chair, Lora nodded, granting him permission to breach the space between them. He settled into the seat opposite her with an ease that suggested he belonged there, a presence that was both comforting and thrilling.

"I haven't seen you in here since that day," he said, a warm smile spreading across his face as he looked in her direction. "It seemed we kept missing each other—sometimes barely."

Lora raised an eyebrow, her curiosity piqued. "And how would you know that we barely missed each other?"

Curtis glanced down for a moment, a shy grin creeping onto his lips. "Because I asked the barista about you."

At that confession, Lora felt her heart race, a mix of surprise and excitement flooding her. He asked about me? The thought fluttered in her chest like a startled bird. Had their brief encounters lingered in his mind as much as they had in hers? Did he think of her as often as she does him? The coffee shop suddenly felt smaller, filled with unspoken possibilities.

"You ask about me?" Lora managed to say, a hint of surprise coloring her cheeks.

Curtis chuckled, his smile warm and easy. "I know how that sounds—believe me. I'm not a stalker, I promise. I wrestled with that decision for a while." He leaned closer to the table, his gaze intent. "But the more I thought about it..." His voice trailed off, and Lora could see him searching his mind for the right words. There was something captivating about his honesty.

Feeling the weight of the moment, Lora decided to step in. "I asked about you, too," she confessed, her gaze dropping to her hands for a brief moment. "Not from the barista, but..." She gathered her courage, meeting his eyes once more. "I was pulling into Ben's Garage just as you were leaving."

A playful glint flickered in his expression. "So, you're the mysterious woman who inquired about me?" he teased, a smile breaking free. "Ben wouldn't share your name with me—just kept it all secretive."

An awkward silence settled between them, heavy with the memories of that fateful day—a moment marked by a fleeting glance shared across a crowded room. It was just a simple look, yet it spoke volumes, fueling a curiosity that lingered in the air between Lora and Curtis, both eager to unravel the mystery of the stranger who had unknowingly crossed their paths.

Lora broke the silence, her voice steady but her heart racing. "I thought about calling Ian at Brooks Construction after I noticed the logo on your truck while you were leaving Ben's," she confessed, her voice lowering slightly as she prepared for the next revelation. "But then I found out from a friend that six months ago, Ian had..."

"Yeah," Curtis interjected, shifting in his seat, the weight of shared grief settling between them. "We lost Dad around that time. That's why I moved here from Chicago just a couple of months ago."

"Dad?" Lora's eyes widened as she straightened in her chair. "Ian was your dad? But he only had one son... right?"

"Yep, that's me," Curtis replied, a warm smile breaking through the clouds of sorrow. "there's just my sister, Sarah, and me." A curious spark ignited in his eyes as he studied her.

A playful smile danced on Lora's lips. "Well, believe it or not, you've been to my house to fish on our lake before— with my husband."

Curtis's interest peaked. "Wait, you're Dawson Bennett's wife—widow?" The realization dawned on him, and he leaned forward, his expression shifting. "I flew in for his funeral," he admitted, running a hand through his hair, the memory clearly stirring deep emotions. "That was just a few months before I lost my wife, Dena, to cancer. That's why she couldn't come down with me." His words tumbled out, a rush of grief and nostalgia.

Lora couldn't help but marvel at the smallness of their world. Here was a man who had brushed against her life, just out of reach until now. The thought made her shake her head slowly.

"I even spoke to you that day after the eulogy," he recalled softly, his eyes locking onto hers. "You looked... different that day." It was a statement filled with unspoken understanding, a recognition of shared pain that lingered in the air, drawing them closer in their shared experience of loss and the surprising connections they had unknowingly forged.

As a hush fell over them once more, Lora felt a shift within her, as if pieces of an intricate puzzle were finally clicking into place. For years, Ian had come to their home for fishing trips, at times bringing his son along when he was visiting. Yet, she had never once remembered his name—his presence had faded into the background of those sunlit days, just another face in the blur of laughter and the sound of water lapping at the shore.

But now, as she sat across the table from him, everything had changed. The air crackled with an undeniable chemistry, a spark that had been absent all those years ago. It was extraordinary, almost divinely orchestrated; she couldn't shake the feeling that God Himself had woven their paths together once more, pulling them from the fabric of familiarity into the vibrant threads of something new. Here they were—two souls, both known and unknown to each other, standing on the brink of discovery.

"Right in front of each other so many times," Curtis finally broke the silence, his voice laced with a mixture of curiosity and realization. "Yet just a face—no name—no connection." It was as if he could read her thoughts, unraveling the tangled web of their shared past.

Lora sat frozen, her heart racing as their eyes locked, an electrifying gaze that seemed to pull them closer, as if the world around them faded into a blur. "But there's definitely a connection now," she breathed, the words escaping her lips like a confession from a place deep within her soul, completely beyond her control.

Curtis swallowed hard, attempting to refocus. "So," he began, his voice laced with raw emotion, "how is Ethan these days?"

"He's good," Lora replied, her heart warming at the thought of her son. She shared snippets of Ethan's life in Texas—his beautiful wife Ava, the lively twin boys Aiden and Noah, now five, and little Megan, just two years old.

"He has twin boys?" Curtis exclaimed, his excitement contagious. "I have twins too—Makayla and Michael! Michael has a son, Cole, who's four, and Makayla has a daughter, Layla, who's two." But as he spoke of them, the light in his eyes dimmed. "I miss them so much. They're all still in Chicago. Michael took over my reins at Brooks Construction's Chicago location; I took over Dad's position here in Georgia after his passing."

Their conversation flowed effortlessly, the hours slipping by unnoticed. Lora found herself animatedly sharing tales of the women's ministry thriving in the old barn, a space that had transformed beautifully thanks to Brooks Construction. She spoke about her cherished moments on the back deck, lost in her journal, and her passion for painting—an art form that had dimmed after Dawson's loss. The pain had made her put aside her dreams, but there was a flicker of hope as she recounted the joys of her creative pursuits.

Curtis listened intently, his eyes reflecting a shared understanding. He opened up about his architectural dreams that had faded into the background after he took over the family business. Like Lora, he had navigated the storm of losing his wife, a reality that sent him into a tailspin, pushing aside his aspirations to simply survive each day.

They gradually shifted to the topic of their children, both feeling the weight of distance that separated them from their loved ones. Just as the conversation deepened, Lora's phone buzzed, jolting her back to reality. It was a message from Destiny, reminding her of their plans later. With a quick reply sent, she glanced at the clock, her eyes widening in surprise.

"Oh, my!" A smile broke across her face. "Have we really been talking for over two hours?" She began to gather her belongings, taking a moment to scribble her phone number on a napkin and slide it across the table toward Curtis. "I really must get going; Destiny is coming over to help me… with some things," she explained, carefully omitting the fact that Destiny was helping her redecorate after dismantling Dawson's shrine.

As they exchanged heartfelt goodbyes, a hopeful spark danced in Curtis's eyes. He promised to call soon to set a date—a real one this time. Lora's heart danced with a new spark as she drove home, her mind swirling with thoughts of their unexpected connection. It felt like a divine orchestration, as if God had aligned their paths just when they both needed it most. A new chapter was unfolding, and for the first time in a long while, Lora felt that something beautiful was about to unfold.

CHAPTER 7

That evening, Lora stood in her living room, eyes glued to the window beside the door, barely able to contain her excitement as she awaited Destiny's arrival. She was bursting to share what had unfolded throughout her day—it was nothing short of a rollercoaster. Just as Destiny's hand reached out for the doorbell, she flung the door open, catching Destiny off guard.

"You scared me!" Destiny exclaimed, hand pressed against her chest. "It's like you were standing by the door just waiting for me!"

"I was!" Lora replied, a dazzling smile lighting up her face as she twirled across the living room with an enthusiasm reminiscent of a giddy teenager.

"What is up with you?" Destiny's expression shifted from surprise to genuine curiosity, her mouth forming an astonished 'O' as the realization hit her. "Wait a minute... you saw him, didn't you?" Her voice was charged with excitement. "Please, tell me you actually spoke to him this time!"

Lora couldn't help but giggle at her friend's eager expression. "Oh, I definitely saw him."

"And?" Destiny pressed, bouncing slightly on her toes, her curiosity practically bubbling over. "You have to start from the beginning—where did you see him?"

Lora placed a finger on her chin, contemplating with an exaggerated look of deep thought. "Hmm, let's see… he was sitting right across from me at The Cozy Corner," she teased, keenly watching Destiny's reaction.

"Oh my gosh!" Destiny squealed, practically bouncing off the floor. "So, did you talk to him?"

Lora smiled mischievously, a glint of playfulness in her eyes. "Well, not exactly," she said, a light laugh escaping her lips. "We just sat there, staring into each other's eyes like a couple of lovesick fools."

"Stop it!" Destiny swatted Lora's shoulder playfully. "Don't make me beg—just tell me!" Her eyes sparkled with curiosity as she urged Lora to spill the details.

Lora chuckled, already making her way through the warm kitchen toward the back deck. She grabbed the two steaming mugs of coffee waiting on the counter. "Let's take this outside." A knowing smile crossed her face as she handed one to Destiny.

As they stepped out, Destiny giggled, glancing at the firepit crackling cheerfully, already ablaze. "Oh, you really were anticipating this talk—fire and all!" she teasingly remarked, sinking into one of the weathered Adirondack chairs.

"You bet!" Lora replied, settling into the chair opposite her friend, her excitement bubbling over. "I had a feeling you'd want to hear every juicy detail." She leaned in, clearly enjoying the moment.

With a mischievous glint in her eyes, Destiny leaned forward. "So, you actually gathered the courage to invite him to your table?"

Lora took a sip of her coffee, steeling herself for the inevitable. "Well, not exactly," she admitted, her cheeks flushing slightly. "We locked eyes the moment he walked in, but I was so busy trying to play it cool that I couldn't even muster the nerve to approach him. So... that one's on Curtis."

"Curtis—that's his name?" Destiny repeated, her intrigue deepening.

"Yes," Lora said, locking eyes with Destiny, eager to gauge her reaction. "Curtis Brooks."

Destiny's posture shifted immediately, the surprise evident in her wide eyes. "Curtis Brooks?" she repeated, the name tumbling from her lips as if tasting it for the first time. "He's a Brooks? That explains why he turned up at Brooks Construction after Ian's death." A moment of realization washed over her. "Is he Ian's son? The one Ian used to bring here for fishing trips?"

"The very same," Lora replied, a knowing smile creeping across her face. "Can you believe the coincidences at play here?"

Destiny leaned forward, her curiosity ignited like a match to kindling. "Start from the beginning and tell me everything," she urged, the anticipation in her voice unmistakable. This was the kind of twist she lived for.

Lora was practically buzzing with excitement as she settled in to recount every delicious detail to Destiny. "You won't believe it!" she began, her eyes sparkling. "The moment Curtis walked in, it was like a scene straight out of a romantic movie—our eyes locked, just like the last time—you know, that electric spark?"

She leaned in closer, lowering her voice as if sharing the most thrilling secret. "And guess what? He's been asking around about me too! Can you imagine? Curtis, the charming guy with a twinkle in his eye, curious about me."

Destiny leaned in, hanging on Lora's every word. "He opened up about his life too. Can you believe he has twins in Chicago? A daughter and a son! Oh, and two grandkids." She couldn't help but smile at the thought of Curtis balancing family life while still being so charming.

Lora's cheeks flushed as she recounted the moment she took a leap of faith—slipping him her phone number written on a napkin. "I know, bold, right? But he took it with that gorgeous smile of his and promised to call me for an official date!" Lora's heart raced at the thought.

Destiny's eyes sparkled with mischief, a teasing grin spreading across her face. "Well, at least you found the courage to give him your number," she said playfully, standing up to head back into the house. "But let's be real, none of this would've happened if Curtis hadn't broken that awkward silence."

Lora feigned a playful punch but missed entirely, as they walked into the house. "I swear, I was totally going to talk to him before he left! I was just working up the nerve," she protested, a hint of indignation in her voice.

"Sure, sure," Destiny replied, rolling her eyes with a smirk that betrayed her amusement. She placed her hands on her hips and scanned the living room, "I thought you were going to get this started before I arrived," she added, sending a cheeky smile Lora's way.

"I was!" Lora insisted, a light blush creeping up her cheeks as she giggled. "But I guess Curtis gets to take the credit for that one too." She reached for the boxes piled high in the corner, an eager smile breaking through as they prepared to strip the walls of memories, to make room for new ones.

They spent the rest of the evening immersed in the bittersweet task of packing away all of Dawson's belongings. The living room, once filled with the warmth of his presence, now stood stark and bare, eagerly awaiting the fresh coat of paint scheduled for the next day. For Lora, it was the bedroom and closet that weighed the heaviest on her heart, a tangle of memories she struggled to untie. Thankfully, Destiny had stepped in, volunteering to join her in this long overdue endeavor—two years overdue, to be exact.

Lora's fingers brushed against a delicate box in the back of her closet, its surface smooth and unassuming, yet it held a world of memories inside. The rings—the shimmering symbols of unity and love between her and Dawson—lay nestled within, whispering stories of their past. Taking it in her hands, she recalled vividly the day she had placed the rings inside that pretty box, the weight of tears heavy on her cheeks as she slipped her own off. The bittersweet moment played in her mind like a cherished film, their giddy smiles lighting up the room as they exchanged vows, each glance filled with hope and dreams for their future.

But the memory quickly shifted to that harrowing day—the day she had gently pried Dawson's ring from his cold, lifeless finger, the warmth of his spirit already a distant memory. The light in his eyes was gone, but the impact of their shared love remained etched in her heart. With a heavy sigh, she closed the lid of the box, sealing away not just the rings, but the essence of their time together. Placing it carefully in the crate, she felt both a sense of finality and an overwhelming ache. This was the end of a chapter—one that had been filled with laughter, love, and unimaginable loss. As the crate prepared to be carried away, Lora closed her eyes, holding onto the echoes of their beautiful moments, knowing that, although she was saying goodbye, their love would forever be a part of her story.

It was the same with each item of his that Lora carefully lifted, she felt a mix of nostalgia and sorrow. Each piece had been arranged with tenderness—as if he might walk back in and reclaim them at any moment. His clothes hung in perfect rolls in the closet, a haunting sigh to his absence. The sight both comforted and pained her, creating an ache deep in her chest. But beneath the sorrow was a flicker of determination; she knew it was time to finally let go and embrace the next chapter of her life.

As Destiny carried the last box to Frank's truck—her vehicle for this mission—Lora stood amidst the empty rooms. They stood stark against her vivid recollections. They echoed with whispers of the past, yet they also hummed with the promise of a fresh start. Her heart raced with hope and anticipation as she imagined the vibrant future awaiting her. It was a moment of both closure and new beginnings, and Lora knew she was ready to step boldly into whatever lay ahead.

"Are you going to be alright here by yourself tonight?" Destiny asked, concern etched across her face as she leaned against the truck that held Dawson's belongings. The weight of the moment hung heavy in the air. "You can stay with me and Frank if you want. It might help you adjust to..." She nodded gently toward the contents of the truck, remnants of a life that felt painfully unfinished.

Lora took a deep breath, forcing a shaky smile as she tried to mask the tremor in her voice. "No, I'll be fine," she replied, her heart heavy with unresolved emotions. "I think I need a night alone—completely without him."

As her words hung in the air, her mind drifted back to the two years since he had been taken away from her. Memories flooded in, tinged with both love and loss. Each moment felt like a ghost that lingered, a reminder of everything she once held dear.

Destiny nodded, understanding the weight of Lora's heartache. "Call me if you change your mind," she said softly, pulling her friend into a warm embrace before climbing into the truck. As Lora watched her drive away, the headlights fading into the distance, a sense of solitude wrapped around her, both comforting and suffocating.

Taking a deep breath, she made her way back to the house, each step echoing in the silence that enveloped her. Entering felt strange—like stepping into a world where the shadows held memories she wasn't ready to confront. She feared that in this solitude, she might forget the beautiful but bittersweet moments they had shared over thirty years.

Lora reminded herself that memories aren't just remnants of the past; they're etched deeply within the heart, carrying the essence of every laugh, every tear, every whispered promise. She clutched that thought tightly as she navigated the familiar yet haunting space, knowing that tomorrow would come, and with it, the strength to embrace the bittersweet journey of letting go.

CHAPTER 8

Saturday dawned with golden rays of sunshine glimmering over the lake, casting a serene glow that sparkled like diamonds on its surface. Lora inhaled deeply, savoring the beauty around her, but her heart was heavy with the weight of Frank's news—the cottage required more than just a simple facelift.

She was transported back to that fateful day when she and Dawson first met with the real estate agent, their excitement palpable as they strolled through the quaint rooms. They had fallen in love with the character of the old house, but it was the lake that truly stole their hearts—a lush, tranquil escape promising countless memories to be made.

Now, as she stood by the lake, anticipation fluttered in her chest. Who would Frank bring to assess the situation? Would they deliver more bad news, or could they offer hope for restoration? The sound of footsteps interrupted her thoughts, and she turned her gaze down the path, eager to greet whoever might hold the keys to the cottage's future.

Would it be salvation or a stepping stone to something new? Only time would tell.

Lora's heart raced as she gazed up the stone-paved walkway, spotting Frank making his way toward her. The sun filtered through the trees, casting playful shadows, but it was the familiar figure behind him that caught her breath. Broad shoulders, a confident stride—Curtis. Even from a distance, she could feel the magnetic pull he had on her, the way her heart always galloped at the sight of him.

Just a few steps away, Destiny lounged on the deck back at the house, her mischievous grin revealing that she knew exactly who Frank had called. Lora could envision the look on Destiny's face when she realized that Brooks Construction wasn't just sending any contractor but the very man who had always sent shivers down Lora's spine.

Lora made a mental note to ensure Destiny paid for this. After all, she wouldn't let her friend slip away from not indulging this information. This was shaping up to be quite the encounter, and Lora was here for every thrilling moment of it.

As the two men approached, anticipation crackled in the air. Lora straightened her shoulders and prepared herself for the magnetic pull of Curtis, a familiar mix of excitement and tension bubbling just beneath the surface. This visit was bound to be anything but ordinary.

Lora took a deep breath, trying to collect her thoughts as she spoke. "Ah, help has arrived," she said, a smile playing on her lips, though it barely masked the whirlwind of emotions churning inside her.

"Yes," Frank replied innocently, completely unaware of the tension in the air. "Lora, this is Curtis Brooks from—"

"Hi Lora," Curtis interrupted, his voice smooth and warm. He turned his gaze to the lake, its shimmering surface reflecting a tapestry of blues and greens. "Looks as breathtaking as ever." A genuine smile spread across his face as he took in the scene before him.

Lora felt a flutter in her chest at his words, her gaze lingering on him. Frank watched in confusion as their connection seemed to spark beyond the casual conversation. "Yes, it is," she replied, trying to blink away the unexpected effect Curtis had on her. She cleared her throat, forcing her eyes to shift towards the water, attempting to regain her composure.

Curtis looked back at her, and she noticed the slight struggle in his demeanor, as if he, too, was grappling with the unspoken tension. He slid his hands into his pockets, a casual gesture that contrasted with the fluttering in Lora's chest. "Frank tells me you've run into some issues—let's go check them out," he suggested, a hint of urgency in his voice.

Lora's heart raced at the invitation. She turned and began to lead the way to the cottage, acutely aware that Curtis's eyes were tracing her every move as she walked along the winding path. Each step felt amplified, her senses heightened, as she grappled with the unfolding situation and the undeniable chemistry between them.

As they stepped onto the sunlit deck, a sense of urgency hung in the air. Lora gestured for Frank to guide Curtis toward the damage that marred the house. She watched intently as they strode purposefully inside, their footsteps echoing down the hallway. As soon as they were out of earshot, Lora whirled around to face Destiny, who was perched comfortably in the worn Adirondack chair, unable to contain her laughter.

"You could have given me a heads-up that he was the one coming," Lora hissed, her tone a mix of annoyance and humor.

"In my defense," Destiny replied, a playful gleam in her eyes, "I honestly didn't expect Curtis to show up himself. I thought he'd just send some of his guys." She giggled mischievously, her laughter bubbling up like a sparkling brook. "Blame Frank! He's the one who called for them."

"Frank doesn't have a clue about what you know." Lora playfully swatted Destiny's arm, her frustration melting into amusement. "That was crystal clear from the way he kept glancing between me and Curtis like a deer caught in headlights down by the lake."

Destiny could barely contain her laughter. "You have to admit, this adds a bit of excitement to the day, doesn't it?" she said, her eyes twinkling as she leaned forward.

"We've got work to do!" Lora giggled, her playful spirit shining through as she bounded into the house. "Help me clear things from the studio!"

As they entered, the atmosphere shifted; the dining room-turned-art studio buzzed with mischief. They were boxing up vibrant paints and brushes when Curtis appeared in the doorway. Destiny, spotting him first, straightened and announced, "I need to go ask Frank about something." She brushed past Curtis, greeting him with a touch of sarcasm, "Hi, Mr. Brooks."

At that moment, Lora felt the unmistakable presence behind her. Irritated by Destiny's slip, she closed her eyes briefly before turning to face him. His warm smile was just a foot or two away, sending a flutter through her. "Hi," she managed, the awkwardness hanging in the air like fresh paint.

"Did you do that?" Curtis nodded toward the half-finished painting of the lake, its colors whispering stories of tranquility and depth.

Lora glanced at the artwork, her heart fluttering with nostalgia. "Yes," she replied slowly, "I started it before..." Her voice trailed off, the unspoken weight lingering between them before she bravely met his eyes.

"I see." Curtis's understanding gaze seemed to echo the unfinished sentence. "You should finish it someday—it's beautiful." Clearing his throat, he motioned toward a chair. "Anyway, I'm the bearer of bad news—maybe we should sit down for this."

The weight of his words sent a shiver of anticipation through Lora. Oh no, what did he find? She felt her heart race as she lowered herself into the chair, bracing herself for what was to come. "It's that bad, huh?" She furrowed her brow, worry etching across her face.

Curtis studied her with concern. "Yeah," he began, his voice steady but tinged with sympathy. It's not a quick fix—and it could be expensive." As he spoke, Lora's heart sank, her mind racing with thoughts of what this could mean.

Her hands trembled as she listened intently, trying to gather the strength to absorb his next words. "It's a structural issue," Curtis continued, his tone now heavy with gravity. "Water damage has compromised the foundation." The breath hitched in her throat, and she felt her heart break as she barely registered what he'd just said.

As those words settled in, Lora felt her face drain of color. "The insurance company... will they cover this?" Her voice trembled, barely above a whisper.

Curtis, sensing the depth of her anxiety, softened his tone. "I've done everything I can to contain the damage, but... It's beyond that now. You'll need to consider your options: complete demolition and rebuild or a partial rebuild of the affected area." He hesitated, gauging her reaction. "Honestly, we can't determine the full extent without a complete inspection. You'll definitely need a structural engineer. I can give you a list of recommendations, if that helps."

Tears brimmed in Lora's eyes as she felt the reality of her home slipping away. "But... my home... I've been here for so long," she confessed, her voice cracking under the weight of her memories.

Curtis felt the weight of her words sink deep, and he reached out, placing a gentle hand on her shoulder. "I understand how much this place means to you," he said softly. "Lora, this isn't your fault. But we need to face the reality of it.

Let's explore your options—what fits your budget and what you can truly live with moving forward."

He paused, his gaze steady and reassuring as he met her eyes. "Would you like to discuss this with your insurance company together? We can go through the paperwork side by side," he offered, hoping to lift some of the burden off her shoulders. The air was charged with both the sorrow of a cherished home at risk and the uncertainty of what the future would hold for her.

"Thank you," Lora said with a sheepish smile, her eyes sparkling as she looked up at him. "I never thought you'd be breaking my heart this soon." A mischievous smirk danced on her lips

"Don't hold it against me," he replied, his smile turning playful. "Your friends are the ones who called me." His voice dropped to a conspiratorial whisper as he glanced around to ensure they weren't eavesdropping.

Despite the ache in her heart concerning the cottage, Lora couldn't help but giggle. "I appreciate you coming by. It's always a pleasure to see you." A gentle blush warmed her skin, seemingly igniting the air between them.

"And I you," he said, locking his gaze onto hers with an intensity that made time stand still. As they stood, Curtis approached her, lowering his voice to a sultry whisper. "Will you let me take you out tomorrow night?" The way he spoke wrapped around her like a warm embrace, and Lora felt her heart race at the soft timbre of his baritone. "Then you'll have a reason to see me again."

"Yes," she whispered, the word slipping out as if it were pulled from a hidden place within her. She felt a rush of adrenaline as her knees weakened under the intensity of his gaze.

Curtis inched even closer, and Lora braced herself for the spark of his lips against hers. Just then, Destiny burst through the door, her voice trailing off as she took in the sight before her. "Lora, where's th—" she stuttered, shock evident on her face. "I-I'm sorry!" Destiny blurted, her cheeks flushing. "I'll look for it myself." A playful grin crept onto her lips as she glanced between them.

Curtis chuckled softly, the moment still lingering in the air. "I was just leaving," he said, his gaze still locked onto Lora's in a way that made her feel like the only person in the room. "I'll see you tomorrow," he whispered, his words wrapping around her like a promise as he turned and headed for the door.

"I'm sorry," Destiny mouthed to Lora as the door clicked shut behind him. Once the sound faded, she grinned widely. "I thought you two were just discussing damages to the house—had no idea you were all mushy in here!" She laughed, dodging a playful swat from Lora.

Lora and Destiny were in the midst of a fit of laughter, their giggles echoing off the walls, when Frank strolled into the room with a curious look. "I wish someone would let me in on what's going on!" he said, grinning from ear to ear. "I was caught off guard by the fireworks down by the lake," he raised an eyebrow while casting a playful smile to Lora.

At that moment, Lora's phone lit up with an incoming FaceTime call. "It's Ethan!" she exclaimed, stifling her laughter as she hurried to answer. "Hey, Ethan!" She tried to keep her voice steady, but there was no masking the blush creeping up her cheeks.

Ethan instantly picked up on the giggles in the background and noticed his mom's flushed face. "Why are you blushing? Is that Aunt Destiny and Uncle Frank I hear?" His tone was teasing, and Lora could feel her heart race.

Before she could respond, Frank swooped in, snatching the phone from her. "Aunt Destiny just caught your mom trying to pay the contractor with a kiss!" he announced dramatically, causing Lora to lunge for the phone in a playful panic.

"Frank, stop that!" she laughed, trying to regain control of the situation. "Ethan, don't listen to him!" She finally managed to wrestle the phone back, trying to keep a straight face. "How's everything there? How's Ava? And the kids?"

"Oh no!" Ethan cackled, clearly enjoying himself. "You're not dodging this one, Mom! I want to know all about this contractor you're 'locking lips' with!" His teasing was relentless, and Lora couldn't help but laugh along, trying to turn her embarrassment into playful banter.

As the laughter began to ease, Ethan couldn't help but shake his head, a broad grin lighting up his face. "It's really good to see you laugh like this, Mom," he said, but then his tone shifted, growing serious as he added, "It's been... a while since I've seen that sparkle in your eyes."

In an instant, his playful demeanor returned. "But now I'm curious about this guy! I might just have to give him a call—after all, he didn't ask my permission before stealing kisses from my mother!"

Lora instantly went on the defensive, her cheeks flushing. "I wasn't planning on you finding out like this..."

Ethan seized the moment, a teasing smirk playing at the corners of his lips. "So, you're admitting to trying to pay the contractor with a kiss then?"

"Well," Frank interjected with a chuckle, "I called Brooks Construction and asked for Curtis to come check out the house. To my surprise, when they locked eyes, sparks definitely flew—so I'd say this little encounter started long before today!"

"Curtis Brooks—that's a name I haven't heard in ages," Ethan chuckled, a nostalgic glint in his eyes. He recalled those lazy afternoons spent fishing with him and his dad, lines in the water and warm sun on their backs. "And now he's pursuing my mom," he added, that playful grin never leaving his face, revealing a mix of mischief and affection.

Their conversation flowed effortlessly as he reassured Lora that he was genuinely happy she had found someone special. Just as she settled into a comfortable joy, he revealed the real reason for his call: he and Ava had a few days off from work and were planning a visit. "We'll be arriving next weekend!" he announced, excitement bubbling in his voice.

Lora's reaction was nothing short of ecstatic. The prospect of a visit from her son and his family brought warmth to her heart. Helping Destiny and Frank put the finishing touches on the cozy cottage felt like a breeze now, laughter bubbling up as they reminisced about cherished memories. Each shared story filled the space with warmth. By the time they said their goodbyes, Lora was left with a radiant smile and a profound sense of peace—feelings she realized she hadn't experienced in far too long.

CHAPTER 9

Lora's day began with an unexpected opportunity—a chance to make a difference once again. It wasn't just a simple task; it was a calling that she cherished deeply. The women's ministry never felt like a chore to her—it was an opportunity to make a difference in the lives of women who needed support. Every morning, like clockwork, she checked her messages, eager to see who she could help today. As she sipped her morning coffee and checked her messages, her eyes landed on an email from Alina.

Alina's story had always resonated with Lora. A new baby that seemed to bring joy yet also stress, and a husband whose drinking had cast a shadow over their lives. Over the months, Lora had patiently listened as Alina denied any notion of abuse, clinging to the hope that things would improve. But this morning's email revealed a chilling twist—Alina's husband had been arrested for attacking her. The words were raw, desperate; she asked Lora to meet with her, that she needed someone to confide in, someone she could trust.

As Lora sat waiting for Alina's arrival, a wave of unease washed over her. She had never faced anything like this, having been blessed with a kind-hearted husband like Dawson, and she silently thanked God that he was a loving man who would never consider such cruelty. The thought of a husband turning against his wife—a mother, a caregiver—ignited a flame of anger within her. How could someone betray the sacred bond of family?

She took a deep breath, steeling herself for what was to come. Lora knew she had to be strong for Alina; the conversation might change the course of her life forever. Each tick of the clock echoed in the silence, a reminder that compassion was needed now more than ever.

As Lora swung the door open, her breath hitched in her throat. There stood Alina, a vision that twisted her heart into knots. The sight before her was gut-wrenching. She stood with a heavy diaper bag on one shoulder, and the baby carrier cradling her precious baby boy swayed gently at her side. But it was Alina's face that truly broke Lora's heart—swollen and bruised in shades of red, purple, and blue, a bandage stark against her skin that masked stitches running across her left cheek.

Lora felt a gasp escape her lips, a sound that felt weighted with a mix of shock and sympathy. The reality of the situation hit her like a cold wave: she had underestimated the depth of Alina's suffering. How could someone endure such brutality and still stand there, a mother, determined and strong in the face of unspeakable pain? Lora's mind raced with questions and a desperate urge to reach out, but all she could do in that moment was stand frozen, grappling with the reality of the situation before her.

"Oh my goodness," Lora exclaimed, her heart aching as she took the heavy diaper bag from Alina's shoulder. "Come inside." She ushered her in, feeling the weight of what this woman must be enduring.

Lora led Alina into her cozy office, a sanctuary she hoped would offer some comfort. "I wish you had told me about this sooner," Lora said, her voice thick with emotion as she settled across from her. Tears welled up in her eyes, reflecting the pain etched on Alina's face.

Alina's gaze dropped to the floor, her voice barely a whisper. "I didn't want anyone to know how bad it really was." There was a tremor in her words as if each syllable carried the weight of her torment. "I thought it would get better over time—I thought I could fix it on my own."

Lora leaned in closer, listening intently as Alina recounted the heartbreaking story of her marriage to a man who had turned into a monster. The group meetings had become her lifeline, where she hoped to unearth the reasons behind the chaos in her life. "I thought if I got pregnant, maybe he'd change," Alina continued, her voice breaking. "I thought he'd see the baby as a reason to be better, to stop drinking. But all it did was plunge us deeper into darkness."

Lora's heart shattered a little more with each word, realizing how much Alina had sacrificed in her desperate hope for redemption. By the time the meeting wrapped up, Lora knew she couldn't let Alina face this alone. "I've found you and the baby a safe place to stay—you can follow me there now," she assured her, determination igniting her voice. "You can count on me—I'll check in every day."

Alina looked up, a blend of surprise and gratitude sparkled in her eyes. In that moment, Lora felt a surge of determination flood through her—ready to stand by Alina's side on this perilous journey to reclaim her life. It was more than just support; it was a promise to help her navigate the tumultuous path ahead

Once Alina was settled, Lora found herself back at home, caught in a storm of emotions as she prepared for her date with Curtis. Her heart felt like a pendulum, swinging between concern for Alina's plight and the fluttering excitement tinged with nerves about her upcoming date with Curtis that evening.

Lora was dabbing on her favorite perfume, letting the familiar floral scent envelop her like a warm hug, when the doorbell chimed through the house, breaking her moment of bliss. With a quick glance in the mirror, she checked her hair—an alluring messy bun, artfully arranged and secured with a large hair clip. She flicked at the loose tendrils framing her face, a smile dancing upon her lips as she admired her reflection.

With a flutter of excitement, she hurried to the door, anticipation bubbling within her. When she opened it, her heart skipped a beat. There stood Curtis, confidence radiating from him like the sun. He held a single rose, vibrant and fresh, as if plucked straight from a garden. Lora's gaze traveled over him, noting the way his white button-down shirt hugged his frame perfectly, the jeans that fit just right, and the effortlessly cool brown leather jacket that added an edge to his handsome demeanor.

For a moment, she was completely captivated, breathless at the sight of him. Curtis flashed a charming smile, and Lora felt a rush of warmth spread through her, the world beyond the door fading into the background as she stepped forward, drawn into the magic of the moment.

"I hope I'm not too early," he said, his grin lighting up the evening and sending a thrill through her that made her heart race. Lora couldn't help but feel a flutter as she wrapped her cardigan snugly around her shoulders, trying to quell the excitement surging within her.

"Right on time," she replied, unable to hide her smile as she took the delicate rose he offered. It felt like a scene from a movie as they strolled toward his car, and Lora's breath caught in her throat when she spotted the striking midnight blue BMW 330i gleaming in her driveway. It was a stunning contrast to the truck he usually drove, and it made her wonder what other surprises he had in store for her.

He opened the passenger door like a true gentleman, and as she slid into the plush leather seat, the warmth of his presence enveloped her. Every moment felt electric, her pulse racing as he settled into the driver's seat beside her. The air was thick with anticipation as he started the engine, and Lora couldn't help but steal glances at him, savoring the thrill of being so close.

As they drove toward Bella Notte Bistro, she felt a sense of enchantment unfolding. The name rolled off his tongue like a beautifully wrapped gift—"Bella Notte," meaning "beautiful night." It resonated deep within her, perfectly capturing the magic of this moment. With every block they passed, the excitement bubbled inside her like champagne in a flute. This was not just a dinner; this was the beginning of something extraordinary, a night brimming with romance and the allure of possibilities. As the bistro came into view, Lora's heart soared—tonight promised to be unforgettable.

Once they arrived at the restaurant, Curtis couldn't resist the urge to play the gentleman. With a flourish, he dashed around the car, his excitement palpable. When he finally reached her side, he opened the door with an elegant sweep and extended his hand, bowing playfully. "My lady," he proclaimed, a cheeky grin spreading across his face. Lora couldn't help but giggle, a delightful warmth blooming in her chest at the sight of him.

As he took her hand and guided her from the car, he leaned in closer, his breath brushing against her skin, sending a delightful shiver down her spine. With a mischievous twinkle in his eye, he nodded toward the softly glowing restaurant sign. He whispered, "A beautiful night, with a beautiful lady—God is really smiling down on me."

Lora laughed lightly, her heart fluttering at his charming words as they stepped inside. As they sat together at the intimate table, the soft glow of the ambient lighting wrapped around them, casting warm shadows that danced across their faces. The flickering candle between them added a touch of magic to the evening, illuminating Curtis's handsome features in a way that made Lora's heart flutter. For a moment, they were lost in each other's gaze, an electric connection that seemed to hang in the air, leaving them both momentarily speechless.

Finally, Curtis broke the silence, his playful grin revealing a mischievous charm. "You'd think dating would be easier in your 50s," he quipped, his voice teasing yet laced with warmth. The crooked smile he flashed sent delightful shivers down Lora's spine, igniting a spark of excitement.

"You'd think," Lora replied with a playful twinkle in her eyes, her voice light but laced with a hint of sincerity. "But it's been such a long time for me that I'm worried I might have forgotten all the rules of the game." She chuckled softly, her nerves easing as the banter flowed between them, like a familiar dance set to a rhythm only they could hear.

"We'll just make new ones as we go," Curis said, a seductive smile playing on his lips. With a playful gleam in his eyes, he leaned closer and asked, "How did it go yesterday after I left?"

Lora felt a rush of warmth flood her cheeks. "I know I was the topic—Destiny already knew—and don't deny it." His laughter rumbled like distant thunder, filling the air with a playful tension.

"Poor Frank was..." His voice trailed off as another wave of laughter hit him, and Lora couldn't help but join in, her heart dancing to the rhythm of his amusement.

Lora let out a soft giggle at the mere mention of Frank. "Yeah..." She breathed out through her laughter, her eyes sparkling with mischief. "Frank had no idea what was happening—I've never seen him lose his composure like that!"

She leaned in slightly, lowering her voice as she continued, "He just stood there, mouth agape, darting glances between the two of us like he was watching some bizarre tennis match. You could practically hear the thoughts racing in his head: 'What on earth is going on here?'"

Her gaze drifted to the candle flickering between them, its warm glow casting playful shadows across their faces. "That's something, isn't it?" she mused with a soft laugh, a hint of nostalgia in her tone. "A connection so intense that everyone around can feel it—A once-in-a-lifetime kind of spark." She raised her gaze to meet his, watching as a soft smile danced on his lips. The candlelight highlighted his features, making him look even more captivating.

But then, that smug grin returned to his face. "You still haven't fully answered my question," he teased, leaning closer. "But Destiny knew—didn't she?"

"Okay, yes," she admitted between giggles. "I might have shared a little about you with Destiny—she's my best friend after all!"

"Everything about me." he added softly, his eyes locking onto hers with an intensity that made her heart race. It was as if he reveled in her blush, finding joy in the flustered way she responded to him.

Lora bit her lip, glancing away before gathering the courage to speak. "Well," she began shyly, "I've told her a lot, but what would I say that I wouldn't say to you?"

"That you're scared," he replied gently, his gaze piercing through her with a warmth that melted her heart. "That you've battled with guilt, feeling as though you're betraying the spouse you lost. And that you're uncertain if I feel the same depth of feeling for you that you feel for me." His eyes searched hers, looking for a truth that lay deep within.

A soft sigh escaped Lora as she took in his words. Dating at fifty was a different landscape; in her younger years, she would have never dared to navigate such intimate thoughts. "You're right," she barely whispered, vulnerability shining in her eyes.

"I know," Curis said, his smile radiating warmth and understanding. "Because I've experienced those fears too. But I've come to terms with them, and I'm ready to take my chances—how about you?"

Lora glanced at Curtis, her eyes dancing with hope as she softly whispered, "Yes." The flickering candlelight reflected in her eyes, illuminating a future brimming with possibilities. "They'd want us to go on living—to be happy." Her gaze sparkled, a beautiful blend of hope and nostalgia.

Lora felt a spark of connection as he slid his hand across the table, gently brushing against hers. "To love again," he echoed, his captivating smile igniting something deep within her heart.

"I never would have imagined that I could feel this way again." Curtis's voice was barely above a whisper as he stared intently at the flickering candlelight. The soft glow danced in his eyes, revealing the turmoil within. "Actually, that's part of my guilt—I don't think I've ever experienced a feeling this intense before." He finally raised his gaze to meet Lora's, the weight of his words hanging in the air. "It's as though God orchestrated this moment, this connection, just to show me..."

His voice trailed off, the intensity of their gaze amplifying the unspoken emotions swirling between them.

Lora felt her heart swell at his vulnerability, a rush of warmth flooding her chest as she realized he was articulating the very thoughts that had echoed in her own mind. In that moment, they were not just two people sharing a space; they were two souls intertwined, reflecting each other's hopes and fears in a way that felt almost sacred. The candlelight flickered again, casting playful shadows, but all she could see was the sincerity in his eyes—an invitation to explore the depths of what lay between them.

As they talked, memories of their pasts began to surface. Lora opened up about Ethan's call just after Curtis had left the day before. She recounted how Frank had accidentally spilled the secret in the midst of laughter, and Ethan's joy when he learned she was dating again. "He was thrilled, Curtis! He couldn't be happier about you," she said, her face glowing with joy.

Curtis chuckled, then shared his own experience with his son, Mickeal. "I asked him what he thought about me dating, and all he said was to be careful," he responded, a playful twinkle in his eye. He paused, a hint of mischief in his voice. "I guess that means I should call him and my daughter soon to share the news."

Lora's smile widened, a mix of excitement and possibility swirling between them. The thought of officially dating Curtis Brooks filled her with warmth and anticipation, and for the first time in a long while, she felt a spark of hope for what lay ahead.

As the night drifted to a close, Lora found herself once again immersed in the soothing embrace of her journal. She smiled, a warm glow lighting up her face as she marveled at how her narrative had shifted so dramatically. Just a month ago, she had been trudging through the heavy fog of grief, haunted by the memory of her husband—his absence, a ghost that lingered just out of reach.

But tonight was different. Her thoughts danced back to the magical evening she had just shared with Curtis, a smile blossoming on her lips like a flower daring to bloom after a long winter. This newfound happiness felt like a vivid sunrise breaking through the darkness, breathing life back into her weary soul.

Peering into the window behind her desk, she caught a glimpse of her reflection—eyes sparkling with life, hair slightly tousled. "Look at you, dating again, ole girl!" she chuckled, the sound ringing out like music in the stillness. Closing her journal felt bittersweet, but she knew it was time to embrace this next chapter. With a heart full of hope, Lora made her way to bed, eager to see what tomorrow might bring.

CHAPTER 10

The following week felt like an eternity as Lora eagerly counted down the days until Ethan and his little family would arrive. Their visits were like a burst of sunshine, brightening her quiet existence in this small Georgia town. Memories flooded her mind of a time when she had seriously considered packing up her life and moving to Texas with them. But as she gazed out at the serene beauty of the mountains framing the lake behind her home, she knew that this quaint, tranquil solitude was where she belonged.

When Ethan had suggested moving his family to Georgia, the offer had tugged at her heartstrings. But accepting that offer would mean starting from scratch on his career ladder. Lora couldn't bear the thought of holding him back, so they continued to share moments that were all the more precious due to their rarity. Lora cherished the laughter, the stories, and the fleeting joy they brought when they came together.

But now, as she sat on this warm Saturday afternoon, Lora felt a wave of joy wash over her while playing with her grandbabies. Facetime visits were always a delight, filled with laughter and sweet giggles, but nothing compared to the warmth of having them right there beside her. Settled on the deck overlooking the shimmering lake, she stole a glance at Ava, her cherished daughter-in-law. Together, they watched little Megan happily playing nearby, while Aiden and Noah cast their lines into the water, fishing alongside Ethan and Curtis.

In that moment, surrounded by family, her life felt perfectly woven together—like a beautiful tapestry of love and laughter. The day had been carefully orchestrated by Ethan, who had arrived the previous evening with a sense of excitement. Their reunion began at Seafood Haven, where the familiar flavors and conversations flowed freely. It was heartwarming to see Curtis reuniting with his long-lost fishing buddy from days gone by. Back then, Ethan was just a kid, probably the same age as Aiden and Noah now, but watching him interact with Curtis, Lora could see that he was fully embracing the moment, even amidst the undercurrents of change surrounding Curtis's return to the lake.

Each splash from the boys, each peal of laughter from Megan, felt like a precious note in a symphony of family life. Lora couldn't help but marvel at the simple joys of a day like this.

Occasionally, Curtis would steal glances at Lora, a playful smile dancing on his lips, one eyebrow lifting in a teasing wink. As the sun dipped lower in the late afternoon sky, casting a golden hue over the backyard they migrated to the charming back deck of the cottage. Curtis and Ethan took charge of the grill, their laughter mingling with the sizzling sound of hamburgers cooking, while Lora and Ava busily whipped up tantalizing dressings to complement their meal. Nearby, the children played, their giggles intertwining with the lighthearted banter of the adults.

"I've really enjoyed today," Ethan said, his tone shifting to one of faux seriousness as he turned to Lora, a mischievous glint lighting up his eyes. "Though I had no idea Mom was getting all cozy over here in Georgia with Curtis—should I be preparing to call you Dad?" He teased, gauging their reactions with an impish grin.

Lora's cheeks flushed crimson at Ethan's words, her gaze instinctively drifting up to Curtis. To her surprise, she noticed a similar blush creeping across his face. They shared a moment of stunned silence, a mixture of embarrassment and joy washing over them, before Lora broke out into a nervous giggle, unable to look away.

Curtis, attempting to mask his own discomfort with humor, shot back playfully, "That's my plan." Lora's heart raced at his response, that simple phrase igniting a thrilling spark that hinted at the doors of new beginnings just a heartbeat away.

The playful banter continued, even as they settled around the table, the delicious food spread out before them. Lora couldn't help but smile, her heart swelling as she watched Curtis and Ethan share laughter over cherished memories. Then Ethan suddenly recounted a story that caught Lora off guard—some summer visits when Curtis had come to town that she had never heard about, trips where his son had joined him.

"What does Michael think about all this?" Ethan gestured between Curtis and Lora, his curiosity piqued. Lora felt a flutter in her chest at the question. She knew that Curtis had plans to discuss her with his kids, but she hadn't had a chance to discover how it had all unfolded.

"Well," Curtis began, glancing thoughtfully at his burger, "when Michael found out I was dating again, he was actually thrilled about it." He paused for a moment, then continued cautiously, "Makayla—" he hesitated before continuing, "well, she's being Makayla. Daddy's protector." Lora felt her smile falter slightly as Curtis hurried on, trying to soften the blow. "It's not that she disapproves of you, Lora. She just wants to make sure I'm happy and that I don't get hurt."

Ethan nodded in understanding, picking up on the delicate nature of the conversation. "So, she just wants you to proceed with caution," he said, offering a reassuring smile as he glanced at Lora. "I get that; I feel the same way about Mom."

Lora felt a rush of relief wash over her as the explanation sank in. She could empathize with a child's deep concern for a parent facing harm—a feeling all too familiar to her. Memories of her own mother's struggles flickered in her mind, a painful reminder of the past. But this was different. She had no desire to hurt Curtis, not now or ever.

As the evening wore on, the atmosphere shifted yet again, with Ethan's lighthearted teasing drawing laughter from

Lora and good-natured blushes from Curtis. She couldn't help but chuckle at how easily Curtis turned crimson under Ethan's playful ribbing. This softer side of him was new—a stark contrast to the poised and confident man she usually knew.

The conversation soon dipped into the troubling issue Curtis had discovered with the cottage. While Lora busied herself helping Ava prepare the kids for bed, she listened closely, concern simmering beneath her surface. Each mention of the cottage tugged at her heart, a painful reminder of what might be lost—the home she held so dear.

Once the kids were tucked in, the adults gathered around the kitchen table, the mood shifting to a more serious tone.

"Have you checked with the insurance company to see what they say?" Ethan asked, genuine concern etched on his features.

Lora nodded, the weight of her worries spilling into her voice. She explained that she'd already reached out and that a surveyor would be sent to assess the damages soon. Just then, Ethan's gaze fell onto the painting that adorned the wall of the adjoining room—a splash of colors that brightened the otherwise dim atmosphere.

"You've started painting again?" A spark of joy ignited in his eyes, illuminating the room.

Curtis turned to inspect the artwork—the half-finished canvas had lingered in the background since he first came to assess the damage. "Wow," he breathed, and for a fleeting moment, Lora thought she caught the glimmer of tears welling in both men's eyes. "You finished it," he whispered, the awe in his voice thick with emotion. As all eyes turned to her, she felt the weight of their anticipation.

"Well," she began, a shy smile creeping onto her lips, "I had nothing else to do." The truth hung in the air. She hadn't just painted to fill time; it was a rekindling of a passion that had laid dormant for far too long. It was a sign—a thrilling assertion of her will to live vibrantly again, to reclaim the pieces of her heart she'd thought were lost forever.

Curtis reached over, gently squeezing Lora's hand in his, a warm, loving smile illuminating his face. It was a simple gesture, yet it tugged at Lora's heartstrings, filling her with warmth. As their conversation shifted back to the house, Lora couldn't help but catch a glimpse of Ethan. He sat there, a soft flush creeping across his cheeks, the tables had turned. Now, he was the one blushing at the innocent sight of his mom's hand intertwined with Curtis's. Unable to resist the moment, she shot Ethan a playful wink, teasing him with the undeniable sweetness of the scene unfolding before them.

As the night wound down, Lora walked Curtis to his car, her heart fluttering with anticipation. She couldn't help but notice that he hadn't brought the familiar truck again. With a playful smirk, she teased him, "So, is the truck just for work, or are you trying to impress my son?"

Curtis chuckled, a mischievous glint in his eyes. "The truck is strictly for work—yes. But I think I impressed him enough when I took your hand in mine right in front of him." They both erupted in laughter, So Curtis had saw him blush too.

In a swift and controlled motion, Curtis pulled her into his arms. Their gazes locked, the atmosphere softening around them like a warm embrace. "I wonder how red he'd turn if he saw this," he whispered, brushing his lips gently against hers. In that exquisite moment, the world outside faded away, leaving just the two of them suspended in time. Lora leaned in, parting her lips to deepen the kiss, feeling the electricity between them surge.

But just as the kiss deepened, he pulled away, a surprised smile spreading across his face. "Wow," he said, his eyes sparkling with a mix of disbelief and delight. "I think that could make me blush." As his gaze flickered towards the house, a hint of a conspiratorial smile came across his lips. "But I think we should let you go back inside—I'm pretty sure we're being watched."

Lora glanced back, catching a glimpse of the curtain quickly drawing shut. "Do they not realize we're both adults and not careless teenagers?" she remarked, laughter bubbling up between them once again. They shared one last quick kiss, savoring the warmth lingering between them before she turned and walked back inside, a giddy smile lingering on her face as she thought about the night they'd shared.

Once back inside, Lora couldn't help but flash a playful smile at her son, who was trying far too hard to pull off an innocent look in the oversized chair by the window. "So, why were you eavesdropping on us?" she asked, her grin widening. "Do you honestly think I don't know how to handle myself with a man?" Her teasing tone dripped with mischief, a perfect moment to get back at him.

Ethan feigned innocence, trying to suppress a smirk. "I have no idea what you're talking about," he said, though his eyes sparkled with amusement. "Besides, I definitely didn't see Curtis trying to make any moves on you by the car."

With a quick swat to his arm, Lora burst into laughter, while Ethan responded with exaggerated kissy noises that only made her giggle more.

"Seriously, Ethan! You're acting like such a child!" she laughed, shaking her head at his silliness.

"And you're acting like a lovesick teenager!" he shot back, his eyes sparkling with mischief as they settled in for a chat before bedtime. It was moments like these—filled with banter and warmth—that made their evenings together so special as they prepared for bed.

That night, as the moon bathed her office in a soft glow, Lora sat at her desk, gazing out into the enveloping darkness. The world beyond her window felt distant, almost ethereal, as her thoughts swirled back to the day's joyous moments. Laughter echoed in her mind, a symphony of shared stories and playful teasing—a beautiful blend of family, weaving together old and new bonds. The warmth of having her son and his family just down the hallway filled her with a comforting sense of belonging, a reassurance that she had longed for.

But then, like a spark igniting a flame, her thoughts turned to Curtis and that unforgettable first kiss. It lingered in her memory like a sweet whisper, a promise of something deeper yet to unfold. Contemplating the possibilities made her heart race with excitement and anticipation. The memory made her smile, filling the quiet room with a fluttering hope that danced in sync with her heart. In that moment, Lora embraced the potential of love and family, allowing herself to dream of what tomorrow might bring.

CHAPTER 11

Ethan's visit had flown by in a heartbeat, and as Lora waved goodbye, she felt the sting of tears welling up. She must have showered those grandbabies with a hundred kisses, each one filled with love, before Ethan and Ava loaded them up and drove away. Now, nearly a week later, she found herself sitting alone, grappling with unsettling news. The insurance inspector had just left her with a heavy burden: they would only cover a fraction of the damage that her home had suffered. With the lake so close, she learned they wouldn't cover full water damage—a cruel twist of fate.

What was she supposed to do now? Dawson had always been the one to handle this kind of mess, and without him, she felt adrift and at a loss. Each potential decision weighed heavily on her heart, knowing that any choice would mean an out-of-pocket cost she simply couldn't afford. Emotions swelled within her, and just when Lora thought she might break down, her phone rang. Glancing at the screen, she saw a number she didn't recognize. Hesitant yet intrigued, she hit the button and put the call on speaker, trying to keep her focus on the piled paperwork in front of her.

"Lora Bennett," she greeted, forcing a steadiness into her voice.

"Hi Lora," a woman's voice broke through the static, one that was unfamiliar but oddly commanding. "We've never met—I'm Makayla—Curtis's daughter." The name sent a jolt through Lora, as she recalled Curtis mentioning her name.

"Hi Makayla, it's nice to finally talk to you," Lora replied, her mood shifting from heavy to unexpectedly light.

"Oh, I don't know about that," Makayla retorted, her tone dripping with indifference, almost dismissive. "I want you to stop talking to my dad." The firm statement left Lora momentarily speechless.

Caught off guard, Lora struggled to formulate a response to Makayla's venomous request. "We both know you're not interested in him—only what's in his bank account. I won't stand by and allow it." Every word was laced with accusation, and Lora could only listen numbly.

"I've already checked you out," Makayla continued, her voice relentless. "I know you have no substantial income. Even though my dad thinks he's found the woman of his dreams, you know what your intentions are—end it now!"

"I—I'm not..." Lora stammered, desperation creeping into her voice, but before she could finish her thought, the line went dead.

The silence that followed was deafening, leaving Lora reeling as a mix of confusion, anger, and sadness washed over her. How had a simple conversation taken such a sharp turn? She felt as though she was standing on the precipice of a storm, unsure of what would happen next.

Lora sat at her cluttered desk, her eyes scanning the insurance papers that sprawled across the surface like a chaotic testament to her mounting worries. The fear of losing her home loomed over her like a dark cloud, and just moments before, Makayla's harsh words had cut deep, leaving a sting that she couldn't shake off.

In a moment of desperation, she picked up her phone and typed a message to Destiny, pleading for her to come over. The simple act of reaching out felt like her last thread of hope. Just as she hit send, the weight of her overwhelming emotions crashed down on her, and she collapsed onto her desk, tears streaming down her cheeks.

Why did it feel as if her entire world was crumbling around her? In that moment, all she longed for was a glimmer of understanding and a friend who could help her navigate through the storm.

Destiny burst through the door, the urgency of her message still hanging in the air like a storm cloud. She instinctively sensed that something was terribly wrong. As she raced through the house, her heart pounded in her chest, her mind racing with worry about her friend. She found Lora outside on the back deck, curled up in an oversized chair, her knees drawn to her chest as she rocked back and forth, tears streaming down her face.

"Lora! What happened?" Destiny rushed to her side, desperation lacing her voice. "Why are you crying? Is everyone okay?"

Lora thrust a crumpled paper into Destiny's trembling hands—the insurance adjuster's letter. Destiny's eyes scanned the page, understanding dawning on her as Lora spoke through broken sobs. "I could be losing my home. I can't afford this! The damage is so severe, it can't just be swept under the rug."

Sitting beside Lora, Destiny turned to face her friend, urgency and concern etched into her expression. "Lora, this is what's got you upset? Frank and I can help you sort through all of this." She laid a comforting hand on Lora's arm. "Look at me, Lora. Is there something else troubling you?"

It was in Lora's eyes—she was beyond just the home issues. "Curtis," she choked out the name, her voice barely above a whisper. "I have to let Curtis go."

"Wait, what?" Destiny's eyes widened in disbelief. "Why do you have to let Curtis go?"

As Lora recounted the scathing phone call from Makayla, every accusation striking her like daggers, Destiny felt a surge of anger rising within her. "Lora," she declared, reaching for her phone. "That was cruel. I'm calling Curtis right now! What did he say about this?"

But just as she activated the call, Lora snatched the phone from her hand, panic etched across her face. "No! Please,

Destiny! I haven't spoken to him yet. I need time to think before I confront him."

"Okay," Destiny relented, her tone softening. "But don't wait too long." She stood, gripping her temples in frustration. "Who does Makayla think she is to dictate your life like this?"

Lora could only draw in a shuddering breath as doubt and fear swirled in her mind. The shadows of her tough decisions loomed, and she knew she needed to find her strength—and soon.

Destiny paced the deck, her footsteps echoing the turmoil inside her. Lora watched, her heart a mix of sympathy and gratitude. She knew that beneath Destiny's bubbling anger, there was a well of humor just waiting to resurface. As she wiped away a tear, she couldn't help but think how fortunate they were that Makayla was miles away in Chicago. Lora chuckled at the thought—her feisty little Georgia friend would probably have turned this moment into a wild country showdown, complete with boots and brawls.

"Seriously, Destiny, come sit down," Lora urged, her voice laced with desperation. "I need the calm, collected you right now to help me sort through this mess." A giggle escaped her, surprising even herself.

"Right," Destiny replied, an unmistakable smile breaking through her frown. "I showed up to be your rock, and look at me—I'm just a hot mess over here." She laughed, the sound bubbling up like a burst of sunlight. "But I swear, if I could get my hands on Makayla right now…" She lifted her fist dramatically toward the sky, and Lora couldn't hold back anymore. Laughter erupted, filling the air between them with warmth, a brief respite from their worries.

"Okay, okay," Lora managed between breaths, "I think we might actually have a chance at sorting this out if you keep that energy up!" The two friends shared a moment of joy, their laughter weaving a thread of light into the heaviness of the day.

They spent the next few hours brainstorming, each suggestion bouncing off the walls of the small room, echoing Lora's growing desperation. The conversation had just circled back to Curtis when Lora's phone buzzed to life, lighting up with his name prominently displayed on the screen.

"Answer it," Destiny whispered urgently, her eyes pleading. "Lora, please," she insisted, the phone ringing insistently between them.

"I just don't know what to say to him right now," Lora admitted, glancing back at her friend, her expression swirling with uncertainty. "If I tell him the truth... he'll take his daughter's side, no question." She let out a heavy sigh, fighting back tears that threatened to spill over. "And if he doesn't? I can't bear the thought of being the reason that family falls apart."

Destiny leaned in closer, intensity radiating from her. "But ignoring him isn't the answer! There has to be a way to untangle this mess. Don't write it off so quickly," she urged, her mind racing with possibilities as the phone rang on, each chime a reminder of the ticking clock and the stakes at hand.

The tension hung in the air, thick and charged, as Lora wrestled with her inner turmoil. She felt the weight of her choices pressing down on her, a battle between self-preservation and loyalty. She shook her head as the ring ceased, "Not right now," she whispered, "I need more time."

Destiny shook her head, her frustration simmering just beneath the surface. "You just can't be serious, Lora." She felt a mix of disbelief and concern as her friend sat there, tears in her eyes. "Please make it soon," Destiny pleaded, her voice softening.

Lora suddenly perked up, a glimmer of excitement breaking through her cloud of despair. "I have an idea! It's perfect—it'll give me time to figure everything out." Destiny leaned in, her anticipation piqued. "I'm going to Texas to visit Ethan and the grandbabies!" Lora exclaimed, her smile shining like a beacon.

Destiny rolled her eyes, incredulity washing over her. "You're sitting here crying about not having enough money to fix the house, yet you've got the funds for a trip to Texas?"

Lora's smile only grew wider. "I don't have enough to tackle that problem right now, but I can definitely swing a visit to family."

Destiny sighed, exasperated but unable to suppress a small smile herself. "There's just no stopping you, is there? Fine, let's get you packed, since it sounds like you're set on leaving on the next flight out."

"You know me too well!" Lora cheered, a contagious enthusiasm radiating from her. As they headed toward her bedroom, Destiny couldn't help but shake her head at her friend's stubbornness, even as a part of her admired Lora's unyielding spirit. Maybe this trip was exactly what Lora needed.

While Destiny helped Lora pack for her trip to Texas, excitement tinged the air. Lora dialed the airport, her fingers tapping nervously on the countertop as she confirmed a flight that would whisk her away at 3 AM. "Perfect!" she chimed into the phone, a smile creeping onto her face. Destiny stood nearby, her eyes sparkling with enthusiasm, ready to take on the Tuesday and Thursday meetings at the women's ministry in Lora's absence. The ladies knew her well, and Lora had no doubts that Destiny would keep everything running smoothly.

After finishing the call, Lora dialed Ethan, her heart racing as she apprised him of her plans. "I'm really sorry for the short notice," she said, guilt washing over her, but Ethan's cheerful voice reassured her.

Destiny and Frank wouldn't hear of Lora taking a taxi. "We'll drive you to the airport!" Destiny declared, determination lighting up her face. "And we'll pick you up when you return!" But as she looked at Lora, an anxious expression crossed her features. "You are returning—right?"

Lora couldn't help but laugh at her friend's serious tone. "Of course! Eventually!" she teased, wrapping Destiny in a warm hug that felt like home. "And yes, I bought a round-trip for Monday."

As they stepped into the bustling airport terminal, Destiny turned to Lora with a half-serious, half-teasing expression.

"Remember, I'm only allowing you to be gone until Monday," she said, her playful tone laced with a hint of urgency.

Destiny reached out, gently grabbing Lora's shoulders, her eyes locking onto her friend's. "Don't delay this longer than it has to be," she whispered, her voice filled with a mix of love and concern.

Lora chuckled softly, rolling her eyes in mock exasperation. "I promise—I'll be back Monday," she replied, a warm smile spreading across her face.

As the announcement for boarding echoed through the terminal, they shared one last lingering look, sealing a silent promise of friendship and return.

CHAPTER 12

Ethan paced nervously in the bustling airport terminal, his heart racing in anticipation of his mom's arrival. When Lora finally stepped through the sliding glass doors, the early morning sun casting a warm glow around her, he couldn't help but feel a rush of excitement mixed with curiosity. As they drove through the sprawling Texas landscape, Ethan stole glances at her, noticing the slight weariness etched on her face.

As the sun peeked over the sprawling Texas skyline, casting a golden hue over their surroundings they pulled into the driveway. He darted out to help her with her bag, but his mind was swirling with questions. Concern fluttered in his chest as he turned to her, his brows furrowing. "You know I don't mind you visiting," he said, trying to keep his voice steady. "But what's with the unexpected visit—everything alright?"

Lora tilted her head, a playful glint in her eyes as she squeezed his cheeks, her laughter light and airy. "Maybe I just needed to see my baby," she teased, but she could feel the weight of his concern. It tugged at her heartstrings, and she knew he wasn't entirely convinced by her playful facade.

As they unloaded the car, the laughter faded, and she glanced away, wrestling with her thoughts. The conversation shifted, and she knew she couldn't keep him in the dark for long; it was time to share part of her dilemma— the little piece about the house at least. But as for the phone call from Makayla and the chaos involving Curtis? That was a conversation she planned to sidestep at all costs.

As Lora stepped into the house, a cozy hush enveloped her. Ava and the children were still lost in the realm of sleep, savoring the weekend's indulgence of rest. Following Ethan down the dimly lit hallway, she caught his lingering gaze— suspicious yet protective—as he set her bags down beside the guest bed.

Sensing that her son was on the verge of an interrogation, Lora decided to intervene. She stretched, feigning a yawn, and lifted her arms toward the ceiling. "I am so tired," she insisted, a hint of urgency threading through her voice. "How about we talk more once everyone is rested and awake?"

Ethan hesitated for just a moment, evaluating her expression. Then, with a gentle smile, he leaned in to give her a light hug. "I'll let you rest," he whispered, his voice warm and reassuring. "But as soon as you wake up—you're telling me what's going on." His look was laden with love and concern as he turned and quietly closed the door behind him.

The moment the click of the doorknob echoed in the stillness, a wave of relief washed over Lora. She dove onto the bed, burying her face in the cool fabric of the pillow, her heart racing with anxiety. What was she going to do?

She had come here hoping to escape Curtis, to find the space she needed to figure things out. But the last thing she wanted was for Ethan to sense something was amiss. If he knew the truth, he would leap into defense mode, just like Destiny had, and God knows what he might do.

She had hoped to convince Ethan that this visit was simply a spontaneous decision, but they had just been in Georgia a week earlier—a thought she hadn't considered.

Thoughts whirled in her mind like a chaotic storm, each worry feeding another. As exhaustion gradually crept in, it became harder to fight it. Finally, sleep overtook her, wrapping her in a much-needed embrace, if only for a little while.

After a few hours, the gentle sound of children's laughter pulled Lora from her slumber like a warm blanket of comfort. It danced in the air, mixing with the faint echoes of playful arguments over toys—the kind of joyous chaos that filled her heart with both nostalgia and a tinge of anxiety. She smiled, momentarily lost in the sweet memories it conjured, but a familiar weight began to settle in her chest.

How long could she hide in the sanctuary of her room? The fleeting thought of her son checking in on her sent a shiver up her spine. It wouldn't be long before he would come looking, concerned and maybe even a little anxious. As the sounds of her grandbabies playing intensified—loud giggles interspersed with exaggerated shouts from tussles over a cherished toy—she knew she couldn't linger in her safe haven forever.

With a deep breath, Lora threw back the covers and swung her legs over the side of the bed. The cool air of the morning coaxed her into action, and she padded into the adjoining guest bathroom, the soft rug massaging her feet. It was more than just a routine; it was a ritual of preparation. A quick shower and a fresh outfit wouldn't just refresh her body, but perhaps gather her courage for the day ahead.

It was time to face the music, whether she felt ready or not. The echoes of laughter continued to pull at her heart, a reminder of the love surrounding her. As the water cascaded over her, she resolved to step out and embrace whatever awaited her. After all, it was time to rejoin that beautiful, chaotic world waiting just beyond her door.

Once she was dressed, Lora entered the kitchen, her heart racing as she locked eyes with Ethan. He beamed at her, a smirk playing at the corner of his lips. "Aww, she's finally awake," he teased, pouring a cup of coffee from the pot. "How about a little caffeine before we dive into the serious stuff?"

Lora felt a flutter of nerves at his words; he certainly didn't waste any time getting to the point. "Sure," she replied, her smile widening. "But can I at least give my grandbabies some love before we get down to business?"

At that moment, the three kids burst into the kitchen, their excitement spilling over as little Megan stretched her arms to be picked up. Lora's heart melted as she scooped her up, showering the children with hugs and kisses. "Oh, my sweet loves!" she cooed while lifting Megan into her arms.

As she embraced Ava, who had approached with a warm smile, Lora's heart swelled with affection. "My beautiful daughter-in-law," she mused, wrapping her free arm around Ava in a tight hug.

Glancing at the chaos of joyful children, Ethan nodded to Ava. "Go with Mommy for now," he instructed softly, a reassuring smile on his face. "You can visit with Grandma after we talk." He turned back to Lora, a flicker of worry creasing his brow.

"Okay," Ethan said, his eyes narrowing slightly as he leaned over the counter, watching his mother hop onto the stool with an uneasy smile. "What brings you here so sporadically, taking a flight in the middle of the night, no less?" Concern etched his features as he searched her face for answers.

Lora took a sip of her coffee, the warmth, a comfort against the chill of the morning. Sliding a stack of papers across the counter, she felt the weight of unspoken words hanging between them. "The insurance adjuster came by yesterday."

Ethan's brow furrowed, curiosity battling his growing concern. "I don't understand," he began, glancing at the papers before searching her eyes for more. "How would this merit a flight—at midnight—from Georgia to Texas?" He leaned in closer, laying the papers down deliberately between them. "Mom—I'm not upset that you visited," he said, taking her hand gently, "But make this make sense to me."

Lora's heart raced as she looked at Ethan, her son's earnest gaze penetrating her carefully constructed façade. For a fleeting moment, the truth bubbled up inside her, but she swallowed hard. Taking a deep breath, she steadied herself. "I know it doesn't make sense, son—and yes, I may have acted too quickly," she admitted, emotion thickening her voice. "But the thought of losing my home because I can't afford to fix the damages... it's overwhelming." Tears brimmed in her eyes, and she fought to keep them at bay. "It breaks my heart to see the place we've lived in since you were just a baby slipping away."

Ethan released her hand, leaning back on the stool as he processed her words. "Okay," he finally said, offering a weak smile that didn't quite reach his eyes. "I'll take that explanation for now—but I still think there's something you're not telling me."

Lora met his gaze, torn between honesty and protection. She knew she couldn't share the troubling situation with Curtis's daughter—not now, not yet. Just as the silence stretched between them, her phone chimed, breaking the tension. It was a message from Destiny, a reminder that she hadn't let her friend know she'd arrived safely.

Seeing a way to escape Ethan's probing stare, she jumped up from the stool, relief washing over her. "I forgot to let Aunt Destiny know I made it safely," she said, trying to sound casual as she stepped away. "I need to call her and apologize for the concern I caused." A sigh escaped her lips as she walked away with her phone, grateful to dodge the bullet again, if only for a moment.

As soon as Lora stepped back into the cozy guest room, she closed the door with a soft click and immediately dialed Destiny's number. "So, I just had a little chat with Ethan," she started, her voice a mix of amusement and anxiety. "He's super curious about why I decided to take a last-minute flight to Texas in the dead of night. I guess I didn't really think that one through, did I?"

Destiny's laughter rang out like a melody. "Oh, Lora! You're definitely not the queen of spontaneous decisions!"

"Curtis is already on high alert, by the way," Destiny continued, her tone shifting to a more serious note. "He's been trying to reach you, but all his calls are going straight to voicemail."

Lora felt a twinge of guilt, biting her lip as she confessed, "Yeah, well, I've got his numbers blocked while I'm here. I didn't want him calling and raising Ethan's eyebrows about why I'm not answering."

"You really thought of everything, didn't you?" Destiny teased playfully. "Except for a solid reason to explain your sudden Texas adventure in the dead of night!"

The two friends erupted into laughter, the sound a perfect antidote to the tension swirling in Lora's mind. They shared a few more giggles, lost in their own world, before Lora reluctantly ended the call. She took a deep breath, her spirits lifted, and prepared to rejoin her son and his family in the other room.

The rest of that day unfolded like a bright, sunny Texan afternoon, free from any tension with her son. Even though her visit hadn't been on the agenda, Ava quickly devised an exciting plan to turn the following days into pure fun. Lora admired how her daughter-in-law could think on her feet. Today, they'd be enjoying a Texas-style barbecue and splashing about in the swimming pool.

Lora was reveling in the joy of the day, completely absorbed in playtime with her grandkids—Aiden, Noah, and Megan. Each shriek of joy and playful splash ignited her heart; she wished she could bask in their spirited presence every single day. Her son was relaxing in a lounge chair by the pool, a blissful smile plastered across his face as he observed his children frolicking with his mother. There was a sparkle of joyous pride in his eyes that Lora cherished.

Just as Lora wrapped a towel around herself and exited the pool, her phone chimed, cutting through the afternoon's revelry. Seeing Destiny's name pop up for a FaceTime call, she eagerly answered and stepped around the corner for some privacy.

"You have got to come rescue this man!" Destiny exclaimed as soon as the connection was made, her voice tinged with urgency. "Do you see him back there, sitting in his truck? I don't know how much longer I can stall him!"

"Shhh!" Lora hushed her, "He might hear you!"

"Lora, please talk to him," Destiny implored, her eyes wide with concern. "Don't let Makayla tear you two apart—he loves you!" She gestured emphatically to the figure behind her, clearly agitated. "He just stopped me on the sidewalk, begging me to tell him what's going on." Just then, Ethan reached over her shoulder, taking the phone out of Lora's hands, curiosity etched on his face.

"What's going on, Aunt Destiny?" Ethan's voice was laced with concern, having overheard the conversation. Lora held her breath, caught off guard by her son's immediate inquiry. "What did Makayla do?"

"I'll let your mom fill you in on that," Destiny said nervously, her own anxiety evident. "Lora, you need to tell him the truth." And just like that, she vanished from the screen, leaving Lora under the weight of her son's intense scrutiny.

Lora felt a mix of apprehension and determination building inside her. It was time to share her truth, to face the moment head-on, even as the afternoon sun continued to shine brightly above.

"Will you please come clean with me?" Ethan's voice was low and tense as he glared at his mother, desperate to shield Ava and the kids from the brewing storm.

Lora took a deep breath, the weight of her thoughts hanging heavy in the air. "Okay," she finally said, her voice trembling slightly. "I had a phone call from Makayla, and she was... very rude." She hesitated, her eyes flitting down to her hands as if searching for the right words. "She insisted I stop talking to Curtis."

111

"Did she say why she wanted you to stop talking to her dad?" Ethan pressed, his worry transforming into frustration.

Lora nodded, her voice barely above a whisper. "She thinks I only want his money."

An unsettling silence fell between them as Ethan absorbed her words. He ran his hands through his hair, pacing the yard as his frustration bubbled. "That little…" His voice cracked, anger etched tightly across his jaw. "I have a good mind to..." He punches the wall before continuing, "I can't believe she would even think that. What does Curtis say about this?" He slammed his fist once more against the wall, and the sound echoed painfully in the stillness. "Is that why you're here? Did he take her side?"

"Ethan, stop." Lora grabbed his arm, trying to ground him as tears sprang to her eyes. "No—he doesn't know about this. I haven't told him yet; I came here to…"

"To hide?" His voice cut through the air like ice, and he took a step back, a mixture of hurt and anger written all over his face.

"No," she shook her head, fighting to contain the unfamiliar rage swirling in her son. "It's not about hiding."

"Then what do you call it?" he challenged, his eyes narrowing as he awaited her answer.

In that charged moment, silence enveloped them, each waiting for the other to break, the weight of unspoken truths hanging heavy between them.

Lora looked up at Ethan, her face streaked with tears, desperation etched in every line. She gently cradled his face in her trembling hands as if trying to anchor both their souls amidst the chaos. "This—this is the reason I came here!" she cried, her voice trembling with raw emotion. "Not to see you so angry, but to prevent anyone else from getting hurt—look what I've done!"

Ethan, sensing her turmoil, reached out and pulled her into his warm embrace. They stood there for a moment, enveloped in a cocoon of comfort, while her sobs broke the stillness, heavy against his shoulder.

"Mom," he said softly after a while, his voice steady amidst the storm of tears. "You need to talk to Curtis about this. He deserves to know what's been going on." He wiped away the tears cascading down her cheeks with gentle fingers. "And just for the record, I agree with Aunt Destiny—don't let Makayla keep you two apart."

A flicker of hope danced in Lora's eyes as she managed a fragile smile, promising him she would reach out to Curtis first thing when she got home tomorrow. Ethan wrapped a reassuring arm around her shoulders, steering them back around the house. "Let's get you back to those grandbabies," he suggested, his tone lightening. "They're thrilled to have you here."

Lora's heart swelled at the thought. She adored being there, feeling the warmth of family wrap around her like a comforting blanket. "You're right," she said, a genuine smile breaking through the sadness. "I wouldn't trade this time for anything." Together, they moved toward the laughter echoing from the back yard, ready to embrace the joy that awaited them.

As they rounded the corner, they were greeted with a chorus of puzzled expressions from Ava. With a reassuring smile, Ethan wrapped his arms around his wife and whispered, "I'll explain later." His attention quickly shifted to the kids, radiating excitement. "Here I come!" he shouted, launching himself into the swimming pool with a dramatic splash that sent water flying in all directions. Lora couldn't help but laugh as she watched the joyful chaos unfold. The sound of delighted shrieks filled the air, and in that moment, she knew this was the highlight of her trip—pure, unfiltered family bliss.

CHAPTER 13

Lora sat on the edge of her bed, the weight of the last two days pressing heavily on her chest. It had been a whirlwind of emotions since she returned home, and although she hadn't seen Curtis face-to-face yet, their texts had been a lifeline of sorts. She had told him she needed time, but the ache in her heart was a constant reminder that she was dancing around a storm.

Curtis, patient and understanding, had texted back, urging her to reach out soon, confessing that he missed her. Those simple words hung between them, a fragile tether that made her tear up each time she read them. She didn't want him to see her like this, her vulnerability on full display through the cracks of her carefully constructed façade.

But today was the day. Today, she would meet him at The Cozy Corner. Her stomach twisted at the thought of the conversation that lay ahead. The café had always been their refuge, a warm and inviting place filled with laughter and love. Now, it loomed over her like a dark cloud, a reminder of the difficult choices she faced.

Lora's heart ached as she considered the road that lay ahead. She knew she couldn't let her feelings for Curtis come between him and his daughter, Makayla. The fear of family turmoil terrified her; it was a line she didn't want to cross. If Makayla couldn't accept their relationship, Lora was prepared to step back, no matter how much love she felt for Curtis. The thought of damaging the bond between a father and daughter tore at her insides, and she couldn't bear that weight.

With every passing minute, her anxiety grew, but she took a deep breath and wiped away the tears. Today was crucial—she needed to find clarity, both for herself and for Curtis. As she headed out the door, she steeled herself for the moment that would change everything. The Cozy Corner might soon echo with their laughter again, but first, they had to face the shadows lurking in their hearts.

As Lora pushed open the door of the quaint little coffee shop, a wave of relief washed over her. Curtis wasn't there yet. Her heart raced as she settled into her favorite table—a cozy corner that held memories of laughter and shared secrets. The air was rich with the scent of freshly ground coffee, but all she could focus on was the rollercoaster of emotions inside her.

She closed her eyes for a moment, heart aching with nostalgia, remembering the first time their eyes met. That electric connection—a simple glance, a gentle nod—and everything changed. It was as if time stood still, and an unspoken bond formed in that fleeting moment. And then, there was the day Curtis approached her, his charm lighting up the space between them as he introduced himself. Their initial awkwardness melted away as they dove into conversation, each word threading them closer together, igniting a love neither had anticipated.

But now, as she waited for him, despair tightened around her heart like a vice. Today felt heavy with uncertainty, and Lora desperately wished for an easy solution to the mounting dilemma they faced. She loved Curtis. Her son had embraced their connection, finding joy in their relationship, just as Curtis's son had. Yet, his daughter's opposition loomed ominously, demanding Lora's exit from her father's life, her rejection echoing in Lora's mind.

The thought of sharing that painful phone call with Curtis filled her with dread. Would he understand? Would he choose her despite the heartache? Anxiety tinged with hope suffocated the air around her, making each second feel like an eternity. Her fingers drummed nervously on the table, and she stole glances at the door, willing him to arrive and ease the knot in her stomach. Today would define everything.

Lora's heart raced as she spotted him the moment he stepped through the door. The air felt charged, a familiar electricity that had always crackled between them. But today, as he approached, she noticed the shadows lurking in Curtis's once-bright eyes. They were dimmed, weighed down by a concern and profound sadness that tugged at her heart—a sadness she had never witnessed before.

He offered a tentative and frail smile, but it didn't reach his eyes. As he pulled up a chair and settled into the space opposite her, the ease of his movements clashed starkly with the turmoil etched on his face. Lora felt a wave of vulnerability wash over her, freezing her in place. The urge to flee wrestled with an aching need to connect; she could see the masculine confidence he exuded was at odds with the grief he concealed.

"So," he began, his voice steady, but crackling with urgency, "can you please tell me what's going on?" His gaze bore into hers, intense and searching. Her heart pounded wildly as she met those sad eyes, the truth crashing down on her—she was the source of his pain.

Curtis wasn't pushing her; he respected the invisible barrier surrounding her pain. It was as if he understood that some wounds needed time to heal, that some stories required gentle unfolding. His eyes spoke volumes—filled with an earnest desire to understand. And in that moment, Lora realized how desperately she wanted to let him in, to share the truth that had haunted her for the last few days.

With a deep breath, she prepared to dive into the depths of her unspoken pain, hoping their connection could mend the rifts life had carved between them.

"I don't know how to say this," Lora said, trembling as tears welled in her eyes. "First—I'm sorry for disappearing on you." The tears began to stream down her cheeks, each drop weighted with a mixture of regret and fear. "I was stalling—trying to weigh the options for this..." Her voice faltered, the words tangling in her throat. Curtis reached for her hand, a silent gesture of support, as if trying to lend her the courage she so desperately needed. "Either way, I can't see…" She struggled to finish, desperately trying to maintain her composure in the midst of turmoil.

"Lora," Curtis said gently, his eyes warm and unwavering, "I love you. There is nothing that can change that." He held her gaze, a fierce determination in his expression.

"I love you too," Lora replied, her heart aching, "But, Curtis—I can't let that love tear a family apart." The tears came faster now, each sob echoing the conflict raging within her.

"Makayla," he stated sharply, sitting up straighter, a flicker of anger igniting in his eyes. "It's about Makayla, isn't it?" He leaned back, his hands resting on his head as if trying to process the situation. "Michael mentioned he overheard a phone call—was that you?" His gaze locked onto hers, searching for answers.

All Lora could do was nod, and soon sobs replaced her words. "I should have known," he murmured, almost to himself. Then he turned back to her, frustration tightening his features. "I asked her if it was you—she outright denied it." His voice grew more intense, anger weaving through his words. Lora sat in silence, watching this unfamiliar side of him emerge.

"My daughter had no right doing that, Lora." He took both of her hands now, his grip firm yet tender. "Her behavior has nothing to do with you." A small smile broke through his frustration. "This is typical Makayla—always stirring up trouble in the family."

A glimmer of relief washed over Lora, knowing she wasn't the source of discord between father and daughter. Yet, her heart remained heavy. What did this mean for her and Curtis? Would she always find herself in a battle against his daughter? The uncertainty loomed large as the weight of their complex love hung in the air.

"So—" Lora let the word drift in the air, a moment of hesitation hanging between them. A tear slipped down her cheek, glistening in the soft light, as she asked, "How do we navigate this? Or do we just walk away?"

"Not on your life," Curtis said, leaning forward, that familiar sparkle lighting up his eyes. "I'm about to face my daughter in a few minutes." Lora glanced at him, sensing the storm brewing behind his gaze. "Don't give me that look," he added with a playful smirk. "This has been a long time coming," he admitted, as he offered a smug dad smile that almost made her crack a grin.

Lora managed a smile, a bittersweet reflection of relief. "I'm glad it's not just me she has issues with," she said, her voice softer now. "But it still breaks my heart that she can't find happiness for you."

"I know," Curtis replied, his expression turning wistful. "It all started when her mom passed. The loss hit her hard, and from there, everything spiraled out of control." He sighed, shaking his head in remorse. "I thought giving her money would help get her back on her feet. But all she wants is money; she hasn't made any real effort to live independently." He chuckled softly, a trace of regret in his tone. "This is partially my fault—I should have drawn the line much earlier."

They continued to talk, laughter flowing freely between them as the familiar flirty spark reignited. Lora suddenly glanced at her watch, realizing her dinner date with Destiny was looming. At the mention of her friend's name, Curtis couldn't help but chuckle. "You've got a true friend in that one," he said, shaking his head with a grin. "She was keeping her lips sealed about your whereabouts."

They both chuckled at Curtis's playful remark, the atmosphere buzzing with a lively energy. Curtis reached into his pocket, pulled out his phone, and with a teasing grin, he tapped the call button. "Excuse me for a moment," he said, casting a sly glance at Lora.

Her curiosity piqued, Lora leaned in, trying to catch a hint of what was brewing. Just then, Makayla's lively voice burst through the speaker, "Hey, Dad! What's up?" There was a lightness to her tone, but it was laced with urgency. "Can you make it quick? I'm getting a pedi today!"

"That sounds nice," Curtis replied, a chuckle escaping him as he looked fondly at the screen. Lora sat in rapt attention, her heart racing as she eavesdropped on the intimate exchange. "So, I'm sitting here with Lora..." he continued, and Lora could have sworn she heard a sharp gasp on the other end of the line.

"Yes, she defied you and agreed to meet with me," he teased, and she could almost feel the shock wave radiating from Makayla through the phone.

"Dad…" Makayla insisted, her voice slipping into a more serious tone, "I was planning on fixing that—I promise."

"Good," Curtis chirped with a grin, "because you absolutely owe her an apology." Lora noticed the change in his demeanor as the conversation took a turn. The color on his face deepened, but it wasn't a blush—it was resolute determination. "Oh, and that pampering session you're enjoying at my expense? Consider it the last one. You're officially cut off—time to get a job!" With a finality in his voice that left no room for debate, he hung up before Makayla could respond.

He smiled at Lora as he tucked the phone away, "The harsh reality of parenting—tough love," he said with a warm smile, his eyes twinkling. As he stood up to leave, he leaned in, brushing his lips against hers, whispering, "I love you."

A jolt of electricity danced through her at his touch as she whispered back, "And I love you."

As she sat watching him leave, she felt her earlier sadness and despair melt away, replaced by a radiant smile that lingered on her lips. In that brief moment, everything felt right, and hope flickered anew.

Later, as Lora sat alone at Seafood Haven, the table set for two, her mind drifted back to the fury burning in Ethan's eyes. She'd never seen him so enraged before. With a sigh, she pulled her phone from her purse and clicked on his name. It felt like the perfect moment to share what had just happened. When he answered, Lora didn't waste a second on pleasantries.

"I told you!" Ethan's voice came through, bright and jubilant, instantly warming her heart. "I'm so happy to hear a smile in your voice again." His words wrapped around her like a warm hug, and at that moment, she was grateful not to be dealing with a child like Makayla.

Just then, she spotted Destiny approaching, and with a quick goodbye, Lora ended the call, a smile still dancing on her lips. "What is that sneaky grin all about?" Destiny asked playfully as she slid into the seat across from her.

"I just met Curtis for coffee at The Cozy Corner," Lora teased, allowing her smile to widen as she relished in the anticipation she'd created.

"And..." Destiny leaned in, her eyes twinkling with curiosity, "What did he say? I can see a spark back in your eyes—was he all kissy-kissy?" she quipped, laughter bubbling between them.

Lora giggled, feeling a rush of excitement as she dove into her visit with Curtis. She recounted the unexpected twist when he called Makayla right in front of her. The moment Destiny processed this, she shot upright in her chair. "Wait—what? He called her right in front of you? No way! Way to go, Curtis!" She threw her head back, laughing, disbelief dancing in her eyes. "Do you think she'll actually call you?"

Lora chuckled, a playful glint in her eye. "I wouldn't hold my breath on that one. Let's just say she's pretty furious with me right now."

"Why?" Destiny shot back, a teasing smirk on her lips. "It's not your fault she's a brat!"

Lora playfully swatted at her friend. "Destiny!" she teased, drawing out her name with mock seriousness. "That's a bit harsh, don't you think?" Then, a laugh bubbled up uncontrollably. "Even if it is true." They both erupted into laughter, the tension easing as they enjoyed their moment together, boisterous with friendship and shared mischief.

That night, as Lora prepared for bed, the sudden ring of her phone sent a jolt of surprise through her. Late-night calls usually came with bad news, and dread nestled in her stomach as she hesitated before looking at the screen. She hadn't saved the number, but the moment she saw it, a wave of recognition surged through her—Makayla. "Well, she's calling sooner than I thought," Lora whispered to herself, her hand trembling ever so slightly as she answered.

In stark contrast to her usual cheerful demeanor, her heart raced as she answered with a shaky "hello," every syllable laced with uncertainty. Makayla's voice came through quickly, tinged with an unfamiliar nervousness that contrasted sharply with the harshness she'd displayed during their last encounter.

"Hi, Lora," Makayla began, her words hesitant. Lora could almost sense the tension on the other end; it was as if they both stood on the edge of a precipice, the air thick with unspoken emotions.

"Hi, Makayla," Lora replied cautiously, her guard firmly in place.

"I know you witnessed my dad's call to me earlier today," Makayla continued, pausing just long enough for Lora's heart to race. "But that's not why I'm calling—Honestly. I've regretted that call to you from the moment I hung up." A nervous laugh escaped her lips, a strange and unexpected sound that seemed to shatter the tension slightly. "I was furious with my dad that day. I'd asked for money, and he flat-out refused. So...I took it out on you. I knew you'd pull back if I said those things—I guess it was just my way of getting back at him." she admitted, her voice softened with a hint of vulnerability. "I didn't mean it, Lora. I'm really sorry."

A grin tugged at the corners of Lora's mouth. So, Makayla really is a brat, she thought, recalling Destiny's words from earlier. "It's okay, Makayla," Lora replied, astonished with the empathy in her voice. "I forgive you. But you really should consider what your dad said and think about making a life for yourself."

To Lora's surprise, instead of an indignant retort, Makayla responded with unexpected warmth. It felt like a weight had lifted, and they chatted a little longer, sharing glimpses of their lives that had been obscured by hurt feelings. As the call came to an end, Lora felt a vague sense of hope mixed with doubt swirling within her. Was Makayla's apology sincere, or just a calculated move to regain her father's favor?

As she lay in bed, the soft glow of her phone still flickering on her bedside table, Lora couldn't help but wonder about the tangled web of relationships they navigated. Perhaps, just perhaps, there was a chance for something more than resentment—and she felt a spark of curiosity about what tomorrow might bring.

She didn't quite understand what she was getting into, but one thing was clear: she was determined to seize every moment with him. His presence ignited a spark within her that she couldn't ignore.

Yet, as much as she cherished the time they spent together, there was a shadow looming on the horizon—Curtis's daughter. Lora couldn't help but feel a twinge of frustration; the girl had a reputation for being spoiled and defiant.

It might sound a bit harsh, but Lora's resolve was unshakeable. She wouldn't let anyone, not even his bratty daughter, stand in the way of the connection she was starting to build with Curtis. Love was worth the fight, and she was ready to brace herself for whatever challenges lay ahead. After all, this was a chance at happiness, and she intended to not just accept it, but to embrace it fully.

CHAPTER 14

As Lora stepped out onto her back deck, the warm sun kissed her skin, and she glanced over at Curtis, who lounged comfortably in her favorite chair. A soft smile crept across her face; it was hard to believe how much their relationship had blossomed. She felt a flutter of excitement as she remembered the first time they had met—how far they had come since then.

Today was special, though. Destiny and Frank were set to join them later, but Curtis had insisted on a private conversation before they arrived. As she handed him a tall glass of iced tea, she couldn't shake a sense of anticipation. "So... what's on your mind?" she asked, settling into the chair next to him, her curiosity piqued.

Curtis shifted slightly, his eyes sparkling with mischief as he prepared to share his thoughts. "You know," he began, "over these past few months, we've talked a lot about the art studio you used to own." He watched her closely, gauging her reaction.

"Yes, I remember," she replied, her interest deepening. What could he be getting at?

"I've been thinking...," he hesitated, building the suspense, "there's a space beside my office in town that's been unused for years." Lora's heart raced. She sensed where he was headed, and hope swelled within her. "I thought I could help you turn it into a new art studio—plenty of room for a gallery and even a space for teaching classes."

The silence that followed was charged with possibility as Lora absorbed his proposal. "Are you serious?" she exclaimed, her eyes lighting up. "I would absolutely love to teach art again!" But then her expression turned earnest. "But I could never ask you to do that."

"You didn't ask," he replied, a playful smile dancing on his lips as he took her hand in his. "I'm volunteering it—this is about your passion, and I want nothing more than to support you in pursuing it."

With a tender smile, she mused, "And how would your kids feel about this?" Her mind drifted back to Makayla's phone call weeks ago.

Curtis chuckled, his laughter warm and infectious. "You mean what would Makayla say?" His teasing tone made her laugh in return. "Michael and Makayla both love the idea!"

"Then okay—Let's do it!" Lora's eyes sparkled with excitement.

As Curtis excitedly outlined the plans for the art studio, Lora couldn't shake off her curiosity about his sudden enthusiasm. What exactly was he up to? He'd been in frequent contact with Ethan and Michael regarding the damage to her cottage. Michael, with his engineering background, was lending his expertise to the project, and today was the day they had all agreed to meet on Zoom to discuss their findings.

With Ethan in Texas, Michael in Chicago, and Curtis and Lora in Georgia, a virtual meeting seemed like the perfect solution to bridge the distance. Yet, Lora couldn't help but wonder why Curtis had insisted that Destiny and Frank join them.

Sure, Destiny was her best friend, but beyond that, she had nothing to do with the intricate repairs on Lora's home. Lora couldn't shake the feeling that Curtis had a hidden agenda, weaving more than just practical solutions into this tapestry of plans. What exactly was he up to, and how would her friends fit into the picture? The mystery deepened, and Lora found herself eager for the call to uncover the secrets that were lurking behind Curtis's motives.

Curtis leaned in, locking eyes with her, a playful smirk tugging at his lips. "Have you heard a single word I've said?" he asked, his tone teasing.

"Yes," she shot back, her smile mischievous. "Just don't ask me to repeat it."

In that perfect moment, as Curtis brought his lips closer for a tender kiss, the tranquility shattered like glass when Destiny burst through the back door. "Okay, kids!" she announced cheerfully, her energy infectious. "You two behave; you have company now!"

Lora straightened up like a guilty child caught swiping cookies from the jar. "What? I'm not doing anything," she quipped, matching Destiny's playful spirit.

Curtis stood, a glint of determination in his eyes as he reached for the laptop precariously perched on the grill. "Now that everyone is here, let's see if we can connect with those out of town," he said, focusing intently on the screen. But Lora sensed an urgency in his movements, an eagerness that suggested he, too, was excited to kick this party off.

Destiny plopped down in Curtis's recently vacated chair, while Frank cozied up on the armrest beside her. As Ethan and Michael's faces illuminated the screen, Curtis joined Destiny, perching himself on the edge of her chair. A grin breaking across his face.

"Hello, everyone!" they all chimed in, exchanging warm greetings. However, Lora's heart skipped a beat when Michael called out smoothly, "Makayla, are you on here yet? It shows you're online, but I don't see you."

Makayla? A jolt of unease shot through Lora. Why on earth would Makayla be part of this call? She didn't know the first thing about house repairs! Destiny shot Lora a questioning look, an unspoken understanding passing between them. Lora merely shrugged, fully aware that Destiny was picking up on the fishy vibe lingering in the air. Something was definitely off, and the night was just getting started.

"I'm here!" Makayla cheered, her bright face lighting up the screen. Lora couldn't help but smile at her enthusiasm, though her heart raced with anticipation. She glanced at Curtis, who stood tall and authoritative, his confidence radiating through the air. A smile crept onto Lora's lips at this unexpected side of him—he was commanding, an embodiment of professionalism that pulled everyone's focus. She suspected that this poise was something he had inherited from his father; after all, Ian had always been a remarkable businessman.

Curtis cleared his throat, his demeanor shifting to a serious tone. "As you all know, I've been in touch with Michael regarding the repairs needed on Lora's cottage," he declared, holding everyone's attention. "With his engineering expertise, I was confident he could guide us on the best way forward." He shifted his eyes to Lora, and she braced herself for what was coming next. "After an assessment, Michael advised that the best route would be to tear down and rebuild. So, I decided to reach out to Ethan."

An icy wave washed over Lora at the devastating news. Rebuild? The thought felt like a weight crushing her chest—how could she possibly go through with that? She looked at Curtis, realization dawning on her: he had brought everyone together for a reason, knowing this would shake her to her core. Lora turned to Destiny, whose eyes mirrored her own disbelief, and shook her head in despair. But what gnawed at her was the mystery of Makayla's invitation to this meeting.

Lora's gaze drifted back to Curtis, who, despite delivering news that was bound to upend her world, maintained his cool demeanor and unyielding composure. There was something about his steadiness that both comforted and unsettled her, a reminder that while her home might be at stake, she wasn't alone in facing this storm.

Lora struggled to divert her attention back to Curtis, her heartache evident on her face. "After speaking with Ethan, Makayla suggested we set up a Zoom meeting with the four of us—Ethan, Michael, Makayla, and myself." Curtis paused, his gaze warm as he smiled at Makayla on the screen. "Michael and Makayla proposed that they cover the costs of demolishing and rebuilding a new house as a gift." He glanced toward Lora, who was bursting with curiosity. Why would they do that? But she stayed silent, absorbing every word as Curtis continued.

"Of course, none of this can happen until after the wedding. At that point, Lora, you and I can stay at my apartment in town while the new house is being built here." Curtis pulled a small box from his pocket as he delivered that tantalizing line. Laughter bubbled up from the other three on the call, and even Destiny tried to stifle a giggle. Meanwhile, Lora was lost in a whirlwind of emotions, trying to process everything Curtis was saying. "That is," he began with a playful grin, "if you agree to marry me."

Lora was so immersed in her thoughts that Curtis's voice faded into the background, each word slipping away like sand through her fingers. She was wandering through her own world, lost in a maze of confusion, when a gentle nudge from Destiny brought her back to reality. At that precise moment, the noise around her sharpened, and she realized Curtis was looking at her with a curious expression, waiting for her response.

Her heart raced as he knelt before her, on one knee, tenderness in his eyes. "Lora," he whispered softly, "Will you be my wife?" At that moment, tears cascaded down her cheeks as she whispered a breathless "Yes." And as the ring slid onto her finger, the word burst from her lips again, this time more exuberantly, "Yes!" As she leaped into Curtis's arms. She looked around, excitement bubbling over, "Ethan, did you know about this?"

"Of course he knew," Curtis teased, an impish glint in his eye, "I had to ask his permission to marry his mom." With a mischievous smile, Lora pointed at Ethan on the screen. "You!" she playfully chided, turning to Destiny, who sat smugly in her chair. "And you too?"

"Okay, yes, I knew," Destiny shrugged, "but it was my duty to help Curtis keep secrets from you this time."

Lora found herself lost once again in the comforting embrace of Curtis, their eyes locked in that familiar, magnetic connection. "Do you have any idea how hard it was for me to wait for everyone?" Curtis murmured, pressing his forehead against hers as his voice dropped to a tender whisper. Just as she thought the moment couldn't get any sweeter, he leaned in and stole a kiss that sent shivers down her spine.

"Back up, old man!" Michael's playful voice rang out, breaking the spell as he called over to his father. "You two aren't married yet!" The teasing made Lora's cheeks flush a light pink, the warmth spreading through her as Curtis chuckled at his son's remark.

Curtis leaned in closer, deepening the kiss with a lingering passion that left Lora breathless, only to pull away just enough to throw a cheeky retort back at Michael. "Maybe you younger men could learn something from us," he shouted, laughter dancing in his voice.

Lora couldn't help but join in the laughter, her heart swelling with joy at the playful banter between father and son. It was moments like these that she knew she would cherish forever, etched in her memory—intimate, fun, and full of love.

After the Zoom meeting wrapped up and everyone had left, Lora found herself seated alone on the back deck, a warm breeze gently ruffling her hair as she watched the sun dip below the horizon, casting a golden glow over the lake. She couldn't help but smile, feeling a surge of pride at how Curtis had successfully orchestrated this little surprise. She chuckled at the memory of her son—Ethan, who rarely kept thing from her, had remained silent on Facetime while she spoke with him and Ava. And then there was Destiny—now that was surprising! Destiny usually couldn't keep a secret to save her life, but somehow she had managed it this time. Lora let out a soft laugh, picturing Destiny's mischievous grin.

But then there was Makayla, a twist in the storyline. She had called Lora after everyone left, to express her gratitude, her voice bright with excitement. When Lora asked her about it, Makayla beamed as she described her new journey—one that had been catalyzed by the fallout with her dad. "I'm sorry for the pain I caused," she had said, "but being cut off made me realize I had to make some important choices." It turned out Makayla had decided to follow her heart and pursue her passion for art.

As Lora listened, her heart swelled with hope. This could be the start of something beautiful—a real bond between step-mom and daughter. She envisioned the laughter and love that a blended family could bring, making the most of their time together. The thought of having two stepchildren and two more grandchildren filled her with excitement.

Gazing out over the shimmering lake as twilight painted the sky in soft pastel colors, Lora imagined all the joyous moments ahead—family gatherings filled with laughter, playful splashes in the water, and the creation of cherished memories. The future felt bright, and she couldn't wait to embrace it all.

CHAPTER 15

Lora stood just out of sight, her heart racing with anticipation as she peered through the curtain that separated her from the crowd gathered in her backyard, an oasis facing the tranquil lake. Each face she recognized brought a wave of warmth—Michael and his wife Lisa, with their lively son Cole, Makayla and Sam, and their bright-eyed daughter Layla. Her smile widened as her eyes fell on Ethan, Ava, Aiden, Noah, and the ever-enthusiastic Megan. Even Curtis's sister, Sarah, had flown in to share in this moment. They were all here, sharing in the joy of this monumental day.

But it was Curtis who captured her gaze—a dashing figure in a simple black suit, his baby blue tie perfectly matching the elegant chairs, the delicate ribbon adorning the arch, and the vibrant flowers in her bouquet. In just a few short minutes, she would step out from behind this curtain and stand before him, pledging her love and embarking on a new life together—a beginning she never imagined she would be writing at the age of 50.

Suddenly, Destiny appeared behind her, breaking the spell of her reverie. "Close that curtain!" she teased, playfully turning Lora around and expertly adjusting her hair and dress. "It's almost time," she said with a warm smile. Then she disappeared through the curtain, leaving Lora standing there alone.

Lora saw her reflection in the mirror that stood on the lawn, and the sight took her breath away. The way her white dress glimmered in the sunlight was magical, flowing softly in the summer breeze like a whisper of hope. The thin straps elegantly cascaded over her shoulders, lending an ethereal grace to her overall look. As she turned slightly, the fabric danced around her, mirroring the flutter of her heart. With her heart pounding and a smile blossoming on her face, she took a deep breath, ready to embrace the moment that would change her life forever.

Ethan suddenly appeared in the mirror behind her, his warm smile brightening her reflection. "You look beautiful, Mom," he said, his eyes sparkling with excitement. She turned to face him, taking a deep breath as a mix of emotions swirled inside her.

"There's someone down by the lake who's waiting for me to bring you to him," he continued, offering her his elbow with a playful grin. He led her to the edge of the baby blue carpet that seemed to glow in the soft light, a path that would lead her to Curtis.

"I can't believe I'm giving my mom away today," he added, his grin widening as he tried to lighten the mood. "But seriously, you make a stunning bride, Mom." He winked at her, and the warmth in his gaze made her heart swell.

As the music shifted, a beautiful melody sweeping through the air, Lora felt her heart skip a beat, anticipation and joy coursing through her veins. This was it—the moment she had been dreaming about, and with Ethan by her side, she felt ready to embrace a beautiful new beginning.

As the curtain opened, Lora's heart raced at the breathtaking scene before her. There, at the end of the shimmering carpet, stood her best friend Destiny, a beacon of support on one side, and on the other, the man who had captured her heart in ways she never thought possible—Curtis. The moment their eyes locked, she felt an undeniable pull, like an electric current surging through her veins, urging her forward.

Curtis's expression was nothing short of enchanting. That familiar sideways grin of his sent butterflies fluttering wildly in Lora's stomach. With each step, guided by Ethan, she felt lighter, as if gravity had temporarily loosened its grip. Everything around her faded as she locked onto Curtis, his gaze filled with warmth and promise.

When they finally stood face-to-face, Ethan gently placed Lora's hand in Curtis's, and the world seemed to pause. The instant their fingers brushed, an intoxicating spark ignited between them, a magnetic force that seemed to resonate through the very air they breathed. Lora could hardly believe the thrill that coursed through her—it was as if every romantic movie she had ever seen had come to life in this magical moment.

All eyes were glued to her, the air buzzing with anticipation as she prepared to share her vows. She had chosen not to pen down her thoughts, preferring to speak from the heart in this moment. As she stood there, her heart racing, it felt as if her words had escaped her entirely. Taking a deep breath, she began.

"When you first stepped into my life, you were just a nameless figure—down by the lake, quietly fishing alongside my husband and son," she recalled, her gaze softening. "If someone had asked me to describe you back then, I honestly don't think I could have. You were simply Ian's son—a mere silhouette in my world."

A gentle smile crept across her lips as she continued, "The day I lost my Dawson was a day I thought my heart was shattered forever. Grief wrapped around me like an unwelcome shroud, suffocating and unrelenting. But then, two years later, there you were—the mysterious man at The Cozy Corner. You never spoke a word to me, just a lingering gaze that held me captive, that charming smile—all wrapped up in a silent nod. I couldn't help but feel drawn to you, sparking a quest within me to find out who you were."

A playful snicker escaped Destiny, and laughter rippled through the guests, lightening the moment. "Who would've thought that day would lead us here?" she continued, her eyes sparkling with emotion. "And I vow to love you with every breath I take, from now until my very last."

The sincerity in her voice echoed in the hearts of everyone present, drawing them deeper into her story—one of loss, discovery, and an unbreakable bond. Curtis cleared his throat; now, all eyes were on him. Lora wondered how he could look so poised and confident under these conditions.

"I think you stole my notes," Curtis chuckled, leaning playfully into Lora. A ripple of laughter spread through the crowd as he paused, collecting his thoughts amid the joyful din. "You know, I, too, remember those fishing days with Dawson and Ethan—and sometimes even Michael," he said, glancing affectionately at his son. "But you, Lora, were always just a shadow in the background—a face I never truly got to know."

His voice grew soft, a wave of emotion washing over him. "I still feel the weight of that day I received the heart-wrenching news that Dawson was gone, not knowing that less than a year later, I'd have to lay Dena to rest as well." As he stared into Lora's eyes, he noticed her struggle to hold back tears, and he continued, his voice thick with feelings.

"But then, everything changed that day I saw you at The Cozy Corner. It was like a spark that ignited something inside me. I can't quite describe it, but I had to find you. I searched high and low in this little town, making it feel even more chaotic than the sprawling streets of Chicago." he chuckled, prompting a ripple of laughter amongst their friends. "It was like looking for a needle in a haystack."

His expression softened as he recalled that day, the warmth of his smile enveloping Lora. "When I saw you sitting there again, I knew I had to make my move. I wasn't going to let you slip away again." Gently, he rubbed the back of her hand with his thumb, the moment wrapping them in a sweet intimacy. "Today, I vow to love you until my last breath, and I promise, I will never let you get away again." The crowd erupted in applause, the air thick with love and hope as witnesses to this heartfelt vow.

Lora's heart raced as they approached the climactic moment of the ceremony. Curtis, with that signature mischievous grin illuminating his face, brimming with excitement. As the officiant announced, "Curtis, you may now kiss your bride," time seemed to still. Before Lora could fully process the words, Curtis swept her into a kiss that took her breath away—deeper, more passionate than any they had shared before. For those few magical seconds, the world around them faded, and the joyous cheers of the crowd felt like a distant echo.

Suddenly, Curtis's playful chuckle broke the spell as Michael tugged at his coat sleeve, pulling him back to reality. Lora could hear Ethan's playful shout cutting through the celebratory noise. "Hey, sir! That is my mother, and there are children present!" His voice rang out, followed by Destiny's enthusiastic cheer, "You go girl! Woop! Woop!" The laughter that erupted from the crowd filled the air, and Lora couldn't help but join in, her knees weak beneath her as Curtis held her close.

As he pulled back slightly, their eyes locked—his sparkling with joy, hers soft with affection. In that moment, surrounded by playful banter and cheers, Lora felt a rush of warmth and love, knowing they had just shared a memory that would last a lifetime.

At the reception, Lora basked in the joyful laughter of her friends and family, feeling the warmth of love woven through the air. She couldn't help but savor the delicious cake that Martha had whipped up; her sweet creations always held a special place in Lora's heart. As she twirled around the dance floor with Curtis beneath the twinkling stars, she noticed something magical about him—a radiant smile and a glimmer in his eyes that sent butterflies dancing in her stomach. Just as she mustered the courage to ask him what was behind that charming smile, Destiny swooped in like a whirlwind.

"Excuse me, I'm stealing the bride for a minute," she declared, playfully ushering Lora away to a secluded table at the edge of the yard. With a conspiratorial whisper, she handed Lora a beautifully wrapped gift box. "This is for the honeymoon—don't open it until you get there," she insisted, her voice laced with secrecy.

But curiosity bubbled up inside Lora, dousing Destiny's warning. She couldn't resist and peeled back the wrapping, lifting off the lid. What lay inside was a cascade of delicate lace. "What's this?" she wondered aloud, trying to untangle it as excitement surged through her veins. Just then, she heard Curtis's voice nearby, "Hey babe—the limo is here..." His words trailed off as Lora realized just how revealing her discovery was.

The sight of the intricate lace had an immediate effect; her cheeks flushed with embarrassment as she met his gaze, wide-eyed. Curtis raised a playful eyebrow, the urgency in his tone lifting just a notch higher. "We definitely need to be going," he said, a teasing smile playing on his lips. Lora scrambled, trying to tuck the lace away, her heart racing— caught between thrill and bashfulness while Curtis watched her with that tantalizing smirk. This night was shaping up to be unforgettable in more ways than one.

"Give me a minute," Lora managed, her heart racing under the heat of Curtis's gaze. As she watched him walk away, she turned to her friend, Destiny, who was stifling a snicker, her eyes sparkling with mischief. "Destiny, what were you thinking?" Lora hissed through clenched teeth, trying to keep her voice low.

"I told you not to open it until you were on your honeymoon!" Destiny giggled, unable to contain her laughter any longer.

Lora's cheeks flushed bright crimson, the color practically glowing in the flickering dim lights of the party. "I'm not wearing that!" she exclaimed, waving the small, beautifully wrapped box in the air as if it were a bomb about to explode.

Destiny, with a playful glimmer in her eye, nodded toward Curtis, who lingered by the back deck, that confident, boyish smile still etched on his face. "Well," she chuckled, "now that he's seen it... I'd say you have no choice." The teasing lilt in her voice made Lora turn an even deeper shade of red.

With a mixture of exasperation and amusement, Lora rolled her eyes. "You are going to pay for this," she said, laughing at the absurdity of the entire situation. Destiny's laughter faded as Lora took a deep breath and steeled herself to join Curtis, her heart pounding with excitement and nerves.

Lora stole a quick glance at Curtis as they said their goodbyes, excitement buzzing in the air around them. A deeper, almost seductive smile danced on his lips, one that made her heart race. Unable to contain her thoughts, she shot a knowing smile at Destiny, her mind swirling with images of the lovely lacey gift she had received. A warm blush crept across her cheeks just as Curtis turned to look at her, his eyes twinkling with mischief, as if he could read her thoughts.

"Let's do this," he whispered, raising his eyebrows playfully, igniting a thrill within her. Just then, he let out a joyful cheer, "Croatia awaits!" With confidence, he pulled her through the lively crowd, confetti cascading down around them like a celebratory rain, each piece a joyous reminder of the adventure ahead.

As they slipped into the waiting limousine, Lora felt a rush of anticipation. Her new life was about to begin, a thrilling chapter full of possibilities—especially with Destiny's unexpected surprise still lingering in her mind. With her heart pounding and anticipation swirling, she took a deep breath, ready to embrace whatever lay ahead.

CHAPTER 16

ONE YEAR LATER

A year has flown by since Lora and Curtis left for their stunning honeymoon in Croatia. Whenever she closes her eyes, the memories come rushing back—the breathtaking scenery, the vast blue waters, and the cobblestone streets she wandered, with her new husband by her side. The salty air mingled with the delicious aromas of local cuisine, creating a magical backdrop for their new beginning.

Now, as she relaxes on the sofa in Curtis's apartment—her apartment too, as they officially have made it their home—excitement bubbles within her. Today is not just any day; it's the grand reveal of the stunning new house that Brooks Construction has built on her property. She remembers the day the old cottage was demolished, the bittersweet ache of losing a place that held so many cherished moments. How could she forget those warm afternoons when she'd hear Ethan's little feet pitter-pattering against the wooden floors, filling the space with laughter? That cottage was more than just a house; it was a treasure trove of memories she had shared with Dawson.

But today marks a new chapter. Curtis, ever the romantic, had kept her away during the construction, longing to surprise her with their freshly built dream home. The landscapers finished the final touches just yesterday, leaving everything pristine and ready for her eyes to feast upon. Lora can hardly contain her anticipation—ready to see her—no, their—new home. Curtis will soon be by her side, guiding her to unveil the next stage of their life together. With a heart full of hope, she let herself dream of all the new memories they would create in this beautiful new space.

Lora sprang to her feet as soon as she heard Curtis come through the door, her excitement bubbling just beneath the surface. "Can we go now?" she asked, her eyes sparkling like a child promised a trip to the candy store.

Curtis chuckled, pulling his still-new wife into a warm embrace. "Well..." He feigned a thoughtful expression, a teasing smile tugging at his lips, "I was thinking we might want to wait until next week."

Lora pulled back slightly, narrowing her eyes playfully as a mock pout settled on her face. "No..." she whined, her tone exaggerated for effect. "I want to go now!" Then, with a mischievous glint in her eyes, she added as she leaned in closer. "Or you can sleep on the sofa until then."

"Ouch!" Curtis laughed, feigning a dramatic gasp. "That's low—hitting a man where it hurts!" He pretended to clutch his heart but couldn't hide his amusement. The playful banter was their favorite dance, and in moments like these, every day felt like an adventure.

As the teasing and laughter echoed inside Curtis's truck, Lora could hardly contain her excitement as they drove through the familiar landscape. As they approached Lora's old property, excitement bubbled in the air. Curtis suddenly pulled over to the side of the road, a mischievous grin spreading across his face as he whipped out a blindfold. "Here, put this on," he said, eyes twinkling with mischief.

"What? Curtis! You've got to be kidding!" Lora exclaimed, laughing but unable to resist the playful challenge. With a mix of curiosity and laughter, she obediently slid the blindfold over her eyes.

"If you can set stipulations about coming here today," he quipped, flashing a cheeky smirk, "I can have a little fun too." With that, he turned the truck towards the new house, heart racing with a mix of anticipation and mischief. As he parked, he leaped out and rushed to her side, gently taking her hand and guiding her out of the truck.

Lora's heart pounded in her chest, anticipation swirling within her. She couldn't wait to see the new house Curtis and his crew had built. This was more than just a structure; it was a dream come to life, and she felt a mix of joy and curiosity bubbling inside her. What would she find waiting for her behind the blindfold? The thrill was almost too much to bear.

As Curtis gently lifted the blindfold from Lora's eyes, a gasp escaped her lips. Before her stood a house that seemed to belong to a fairy tale—elegant and breathtaking. The rich, dark-toned wood blended seamlessly with the sleek stone façade, while the expansive glass windows beckoned with their shimmering reflections, sparkling like jewels in the afternoon sun.

Lora felt her heart race as she stepped forward, her feet moving almost of their own accord toward the grand front door. The door itself was a work of art, adorned with an oval stained glass piece that caught the sunlight, illuminating the entryway with vibrant colors that danced across the ground.

She stood there, awestruck and speechless, as Curtis beamed with pride beside her. Every inch of the house radiated warmth and personality, inviting her into what felt like an enchanting dream. In that moment, Lora was captivated by its beauty.

Lora's breath caught in her throat as Curtis whisked her away from the doorknob, effortlessly lifting her into his arms. "Allow me the honor," he said, his eyes sparkling with joy and mischief. As he opened the door, the anticipation hung thick in the air. He leaned in and gave her a soft, lingering kiss before gently setting her down on her feet.

As she turned, the first words spilled from her mouth, her excitement palpable, "Oh my gosh!" she exclaimed, her voice filled with wonder. "What a view!" She glanced back at Curtis, who stood behind her, his charming smile radiating warmth and love

It was the impressive floor-to-ceiling windows lining the back wall that first captured her attention, reflecting the lake's shimmering surface just beyond. The expansive glass panes welcomed abundant natural light, bathing the interior in a warm glow and creating an airy, inviting atmosphere that felt alive. Lora's heart soared as she took in the open-concept design, where fresh lines and a soothing neutral color palette merged with elegance.

As her gaze traveled through the space, she noticed how the living area seamlessly flowed into a modern kitchen, equipped with state-of-the-art appliances and a large island that beckoned for casual gatherings and shared moments. The scene was nothing short of magical, and Lora felt a wave of joy wash over her. This was more than just a home; it was a breathtaking sanctuary, a dream come to life.

As Lora ventured deeper into the house, she marveled at how each room had been thoughtfully positioned to frame breathtaking views of the shimmering lake, making the beauty of nature an integral part of everyday life. The bedrooms, designed as serene sanctuaries, boasted expansive windows or sliding doors that opened onto private balconies—imagine starting each day with the soothing sounds of water gently cascading against the shore, sunlight dancing through the leaves overhead. Even the his-and-hers offices offered that same serene panorama, blending productivity with peaceful scenery.

Stepping outside onto a spacious deck, Lora felt a wave of tranquility wash over her as she took in the vista of the water. This was the perfect space for lively outdoor gatherings or quiet mornings where she could sip her coffee while basking in the sun's warmth. Surrounded by plush seating and featuring a fire pit, the deck transformed into a cozy haven for evening moments with her husband, where they could exchange stories and laugh under a blanket of stars. The allure of the lake seemed to promise new memories waiting to be made.

As Lora stood on the deck, breathing in the fresh scent of the lake, the scene before her was nothing short of magical. The shimmering water mirrored the sky's hues, casting a serene spell that made her heart swell. Just then, she felt a warm presence behind her; Curtis stepped in close, wrapping his arms around her waist with a familiarity that felt like home. "What are you thinking?" he whispered, their bodies swaying gently to the rhythm of the soft breeze that danced around them. "I take it you don't like the house— you haven't said much since we arrived," he added, a teasing grin flickering on his lips.

Startled, Lora spun around to face him, her eyes wide with surprise. "Are you out of your mind?" she exclaimed, the corners of her lips turning up as she caught the playful glimmer in his gaze. "I haven't said anything because it's absolutely breathtaking!" Curtis leaned down, planting a soft kiss on her forehead, a gesture that made her heart flutter. She gazed up at him, "Who came up with the floor plan?" she asked, curiosity lighting up her face.

"You did," he replied with mock seriousness, "I remembered how much you love this lake—I wanted it to be the focal point of your life." Their gazes held, and in that moment, Lora felt an overwhelming rush of love for this man who was a dream come true.

A proud smile spread across Curtis's face as he leaned against the railing, his eyes sparkling with excitement. "But...," he began, his voice warm and inviting, "pulling it all together was a team effort." He paused, a glint of excitement in his eyes. "Ethan told us all those stories you've woven through the years about your ideal home—the one with walls of windows, allowing you to soak in that breathtaking view every single day."

"And then," he continued, a hint of pride creeping into his tone. "Michael and I rolled up our sleeves, drafted the blueprints, and then sent the crew into action. But the real magic? That's all Makayla. She's the genius behind those whimsical solar fairy lights that twinkle around the lake, illuminating the path and adding magic to the landscape. It's her creativity that brought it all together!"

Curtis turned his gaze back to her, his smile warm and full of love. "It's not just a house—it's a dream realized, thanks to everyone coming together." The air was charged with excitement as she absorbed every word, feeling the love and effort that had woven this dream into reality.

Just as he leaned in, ready to deepen the moment, Destiny burst through the back door, her energy bright as a summer day. "Lora! This house is absolutely beaut—" Her words faltered as she noticed them, and a mischievous smile stretched across her face. "Can you two exist without your lips glued together?" she teased, sinking into one of the new plush chairs and letting out a satisfied sigh, running her hand over its soft surface, momentarily lost in its comfort.

"Hi, Destiny!" Lora giggled. "Come on in and make yourself at home." Destiny didn't respond as she was lost in the moment of admiring Lora's new home.

Destiny propped herself up, her eyes sparkling with an idea. "Why don't we break in this new deck tonight?" she mused. "How about a little housewarming party?" Her gaze flickered between the two of them, seeking their approval.

Before Lora could respond, Curtis chimed in, "That's not a bad idea." He turned to Lora, his expression lighting up with excitement. "I know you'd want to stay here tonight—let's invite Destiny and Frank over for a cookout." He nodded at Destiny, who practically sparkled with enthusiasm at the thought.

Lora's eyes lit up, a contagious thrill coursing through her. "Let's do it!" she exclaimed, wrapping her arms around her husband's neck, her heart racing with anticipation.

"Okay, okay!" Destiny chirped, springing up from her seat like a firework. "You two hold off on the kissing until I leave!" She shot them a playful smirk before heading toward the door. "I'll go round up Frank and be back around... say, 5?"

Curtis and Lora nodded in agreement, and just as their lips met in a passionate kiss, Destiny shook her head in exaggerated disbelief. "You two—I swear," she called out with a laugh, disappearing through the door, leaving the couple basking in their shared happiness and the promise of a wonderful evening ahead.

As the day unfolded, it revealed more surprises than Lora or Curtis had ever anticipated. Their kids—both his and hers—had orchestrated a delightful surprise visit, bringing along all the grandbabies.

Lora settled into the comforting embrace of her husband on the spacious lounge of their deck, a picturesque setting that felt almost magical. She glanced over at the bustling scene: kids running, laughter ringing out, and the little ones chasing each other with pure delight.

As she gazed upon their lively family—Destiny and Frank included—her heart swelled with gratitude. She turned to Curtis, noticing the warmth in his eyes, reflecting the same joy that surged within her. "What are you thinking?" he whispered, his voice gentle and inviting.

"Life is perfect right now," she replied, a radiant smile gracing her lips.

He leaned in, planting a soft kiss on her forehead, the intimacy of the moment making her heart flutter. "This is what all those extra rooms were for," he murmured, grinning. "One for each grown child and their families—and one for friends who feel like family." They shared a quiet chuckle, the kind that spoke volumes of their bond.

Lora nestled back against him, her heart swelling with joy. She felt incredibly blessed—God had gifted her not only a wonderful man but also a fabulous best friend and a vibrant, blended family filled with laughter and love. She took a moment to look up at the sprawling night sky, her thoughts drifting to Dawson and Dena. She could almost sense their smiles beaming down on them, sharing in this beautiful tapestry of family that had been woven with care and love. It was a perfect moment, one she would cherish forever.

ABOUT THE AUTHOR

Karen Pless Gaines is a contemporary Christian romance novelist who writes stories that explore themes of faith, hope, and healing. Drawing inspiration from her own life experiences and a strong commitment to sharing stories of resilience and redemption, she aims to provide readers with uplifting and inspirational narratives. In addition to fiction, she also writes non-fiction books on spiritual growth. When she isn't writing, Karen enjoys spending time with her family, working in the women's ministry, and crafting. You can contact her on Facebook at @authorkpgaines for more information about her books and upcoming projects.

You can find more amazing books by Karen on Amazon

https://www.amazon.com/author/karenplessgaines

On Goodreads

https://www.goodreads.com/authorkpgaines